STORM

INTERGALACTIC DATING AGENCY

DRAGON BRIDES
BOOK 5

KATE RUDOLPH

Storm © Kate Rudolph 2022.

Published by Kate Rudolph.
www.katerudolph.net

ABOUT THE BOOK

He's not looking for a mate…

Dragon lord Storm is under an ultimatum: find a bride or lose his inheritance. But he is no man to be pushed around. When a matchmaker instructs him where to look for his mate, he's determined to refuse.

Unfortunately some orders must be followed. Especially when they come from the king. And when he sets eyes on River, a human woman from a diplomatic delegation, he's determined to make her his own.

It's a simple enough plan. Until an attack puts River, Storm, and two diplomatic delegations in danger. With only River to rely on, Storm will find exactly what his mate is made of.

But can he convince his strong and feisty human to rely on him and accept him as her mate?

CHAPTER
ONE

DRAGON LORD STORM was not the most patient of all his brothers. That fact had spread across the kingdom like lightning during his school days when he'd had even less control over his temper than he did as a man. Some had claimed his name was apt. A dragon in a foul temper was surrounded by his own smoke, and it could appear like storm clouds circling a man.

Today Storm moved too fast for his smoke to gather in one place. It trailed after him and made his path clear.

The cliff overlooked the sea at the edge of his property. He could jump now, shift into his other form and fly for days without seeing another being. He'd tried it once. The sea stretched on and on and on. He'd flown so far that he'd feared he'd need a rescue, but endurance and hardheadedness had seen him home.

But how would it get him out of this mess?

His mother was an exacting woman. She wanted each of her sons to live up to the image she had for them. And as the second son, Storm had failed more often than he succeeded.

But she'd never gone this far.

"Wait up, Storm!" he heard a voice call from some distance behind him.

Storm turned and there was Drake, his younger brother. He was jogging to catch up and waving a hand in front of his face to clear the smoke.

"I thought for sure you'd jump to avoid me," he said, coughing a bit as the smoke began to clear. "Luckily I'm faster, you'd never get away." He bumped his shoulder against Storm's.

Storm wouldn't dignify that with a glare. "Perhaps if one of my wings were torn off."

Drake laughed, but it cut off sooner than it should have, and he sighed. "I'm surprised you didn't speak your mind back there."

Storm bit back a snarl. "And lose my inheritance then and there? I've no need to be her sole heir, but I'd rather *not* be put on the street."

"As if you don't have a hoard of gold hidden some-where?" Drake challenged with a faint smile.

Storm shrugged, unmoved by his brother's teasing.

"It's the same for all of us. But whoever she chooses will have control of the rest."

"And be under her thumb for the next few decades." Drake sounded bitter.

"You've been looking for a bride for ages. Are you so disappointed now your hand has been forced?" Storm had watched his brother dance attendance on dozens of appropriate ladies over the last few years, and he'd even thought the man had come close to a betrothal a time or two. "What about Cinda?"

His brother actually *growled*. "Apparently I'm not exciting enough for the lady. I disappointed her by refusing to duel another dragon for her favor." He kicked a pebble on the ground and they both watched it fly over the edge of the cliff.

Storm didn't know what to say. Drake had been on the lookout for love since he'd become a man. That he had yet to find it made Storm wonder if such a thing even existed. Sure, he'd seen plenty of happily paired off dragons, but what a person saw on the outside and what was real were often very different.

"If she didn't see your worth, she isn't for you," he finally said. "Perhaps Mother's edict will work out for you. You've never seen the matchmaker, have you?"

Drake groaned. "I had hoped to find my way on my own," he said, but then he shook himself. "Though the matchmaker may be exactly what we need."

"Suit yourself, brother. I'm not meeting with her."

He'd been sure of that the moment his mother's assistant sent him a notification of his appointment.

"What?" Drake was shocked, and Storm knew why. It was one thing to circumvent their mother's wishes. Ignoring them entirely led to trouble.

But Storm *couldn't.* Two hours ago, he'd sat in his mother's main receiving room and listened to her ultimatum. She was leaving the planet for a year to act as the king's representative at a distant dragon colony. When she returned, she expected each of her sons to be wed. Whoever she deemed to have the most appropriate match would be named her heir.

The others would be left to rot.

Well, she hadn't said that last bit out loud. But it had been implied. Heavily.

"Even Cipher is going to his meeting. You have to." Drake looked around wildly as if he feared their mother might have spies of some sort in the field with them.

She was good, but she wasn't that good.

Storm hadn't bothered to find out what his older brother had to say about the matter. Cipher had been in line to be the heir since birth. He wouldn't let something like this stop him. If a proper marriage was required, he'd marry properly.

So really, Storm didn't have to bother. The inheritance was settled already.

"It isn't just the family estates," Drake pointed out.

"Mother is connected to every noble in the kingdom. If she becomes insistent…"

"If?" Storm's dragon screamed to be let out of his skin. He needed to fly, needed to escape these expectations. He couldn't impress his mother. He couldn't remember a time in his thirty-three years where she'd been truly happy with him.

He wasn't about to start now.

"At least consider it." Drake grabbed his arm and gave it a squeeze before quickly letting it drop.

Storm looked out over the raging sea and felt something spark in his soul. "I'm going for a flight." And before his brother could stop him or offer to join, he took two running steps and launched himself over the edge of the cliff, shifting to his other form in mid-air.

The worries about his future slid away, not completely gone, but nestled in the back of his mind where he could ignore them. In the air there were no sharp mothers ready to skewer him with expectations. No, here he was as free as any dragon ever was.

He flew out until he could no longer see the shore and glided on air currents, diving down until his wings skimmed the roiling water before pumping up and into the air again.

No one joined him. For that small amount of time, he was on his own private planet. No rules, no expectations, no future.

But Storm couldn't stay in the air all night. In the

distance the clouds churned, threatening to open up the skies in battering winds and rain. And while he liked a challenge, flying during a squall took the kind of focus he didn't currently possess.

He winged back to town and shifted, walking the rest of the way to one of his favorite taverns as the sun set. The sky grew heavier by the moment and it released its fury just as he ducked inside.

The tavern was lively, full of dragons out for a night of fun.

In a blink, Storm had a tankard of ale in his hands and was swallowed up by a group of jolly dragons laughing about the antics a pack of dragonlings had gotten into earlier that day. He had nothing to share, but no one minded, and as the night went on, he let his worries melt away.

The ale had dulled the edges of his anger by the time he took a seat in a corner and let him observe the revelry. And when a beautiful woman sat at his table, he smiled.

She was a bit older than him, with light brown skin, hair obscured by a scarf, and striking blue eyes. "My lord, I was told you'd keep your appointments."

And just like that, his mood soured again. He'd only had one appointment to keep, and it was happily skipped. "And you are?" But as he asked, he feared he already knew.

She reached into a pocket and pulled out a card. It

read SHADE | ROYAL MATCHMAKER, and in smaller text at the bottom of the card he could just make out the letters IDA.

He couldn't care enough to ask what they meant. "I saw no reason to waste your time." Rumor said the matchmaker was some kind of psychic. She could spot a dragon's mate across an entire galaxy.

It sounded like excellent marketing. Storm didn't buy it.

"You did, Lord Storm, but I'm giving you another chance. Listen to me or don't, but I shall not waste my gift." She raised a brow, daring him to send her away.

Despite himself, Storm was intrigued. He sat and waited for her to continue, somehow reasoning that all would be well so long as he didn't *actively* seek her advice.

"To meet your mate, obey the king's next request," she told him. "Disobey at your own peril."

"Is *that* what you're paid for?" he scoffed. If making absurd and obvious statements had the world thinking Shade was a psychic, Storm was sure he could do it himself.

Shade stood and offered a small bow. "Have fun, my lord. And safe travels." Without another word, she was off.

Storm gripped his tankard and glared. He didn't need a mate. And he wouldn't let his life be ruled by some fraudulent psychic.

CHAPTER
TWO

"YOU CAN DO THIS. It's going to be alright." River clutched her hands at her sides as she paced back and forth in her bedroom.

Outside she could hear the children of Mayt giggling as they played some game on the small play area right outside the school. Until last week, she'd been a teacher there along with so many of the other young women in her city.

Now she was going to be a diplomat.

If she didn't throw up.

She seized a bit of courage and strode out the door, leaving her room in a bit of a mess. It was fine. She'd tidy before she left.

She was going into space!

Excitement sizzled in her veins as she trailed her fingers along one of the walls of the narrow hallway.

She'd been to the small space station that was in orbit above the city, but never dreamed she'd go farther.

And she'd never imagined she would meet a *dragon*.

But it was all happening. Simply because she'd been brave enough to put her name forward.

"Seth's looking for you," Juniper, a kindly older woman with long blonde hair and wise eyes told her as she passed River in the hallway. "He sounded urgent."

River's eyes widened. "Thanks!" They were leaving in two days and she wasn't going to mess this up by disappointing her leader before they lifted off. Seth had chosen her specifically out of all the non-diplomats who'd applied. He'd told her she had something special about her.

She was going to make him proud.

She rushed through the hallway and out onto the path that would lead her to the diplomatic offices. It was a small building. Mayt wasn't a large settlement, and for the past century or so they'd mostly kept to themselves.

But that was all changing now.

There were other people out in the stars. Civilizations and empires, forces for good and for evil. And if Mayt didn't start making friends, then all they'd have to look forward to was being swiftly swallowed up by some power they couldn't comprehend.

And that was where the dragons of Vemion came

in. Mayt was a human settlement and the planet was still mostly uninhabited outside of three large cities. Dragons could come and fly for days without any sort of interference, and then seek out the cities for the entertainment they provided.

And the humans wanted to go to Vemion. Ever since rumors of a dragon planet had reached the populace, there had been whispers that were growing into louder demands.

So now Mayt wanted a treaty of friendship and to open up travel between their two planets. It would be the first such treaty that Mayt entered into.

If River did this right.

And maybe one day the diplomatic office would grow bigger.

She darted down the hall to the corner office that Seth had claimed as his own and knocked on the open door.

Seth beckoned her in with a smile. "Shut the door, will you?" he asked. He was about twenty years older than her and had been working in the Mayt government for as long as she could remember. He had kind eyes that were set deep into growing wrinkles and dark hair that was beginning to gray at the temples. And he was short. It was something that always put River at ease about him; they were the same height and had been since she was thirteen.

She took a seat opposite his desk. "Juniper said you

were looking for me?" What could this be for? "The mission is still on, right? I'm still going?" Her heartbeat shot up at the idea it might be scrapped so close to takeoff. This was her *chance*.

Seth waved a hand to calm her. "Of course. I thought we'd go over a few items while we have time. To make sure you're truly ready."

River nodded eagerly and leaned forward. "I'm almost completely packed. I can't wait."

"Good, good." Seth pushed a few papers her way. "I've added a bit of data to the profiles of the dignitaries we'll be meeting. I think you should pay special attention to Lord Storm. He's the youngest of them, not much older than you, and single. Rumor has it he's very open with his affection."

She didn't reach for the paper, instead looking at Seth. "What?" Her stomach sank as she realized exactly why Seth might have chosen to bring a pretty young woman on this trip when he'd been so adamantly against it until recently.

He nudged the paper again. "We need every advantage we can get, Miss Maid. Or do you want this mission to fall through because you could not send a few friendly smiles to an aristocrat?"

"Don't put this on me!" She wanted to storm out of the room and declare she wouldn't go on the mission if they begged her. But this mission was her dream. It was the start of big things. And Seth hadn't actually asked her to do anything… untoward. "You just want me to flirt? Me?" Suitors weren't exactly heavy on the ground around her, and the last time she'd tried to flirt with a man he'd ended up taking her friend Kylar out on a date instead.

Seth pushed on the paper again until it was hanging off the desk. "I want you to do what needs to be done for this mission. If you can't do that, I'll find someone else."

Alarm zinged through her. She wasn't going to prostitute herself out just to make the dragons sweet. But she could be free with her smiles. That was the job. "It's fine, sir. I'll do what I need to."

"You better."

There was a knock on the door and it opened before Seth could say anything. Ash Master, another member of their crew, stuck his head in. "You ready for the meeting with Luke and Will?" he asked.

Luke and Will, that rounded out the diplomatic crew.

"We have a meeting?" she asked, looking between Seth and Ash.

"*We* have a meeting," Seth told her as he stood and nodded towards Ash. "Think about what I've said and make sure your head is on straight. Come on." He wasn't about to leave her alone in his office where he kept highly confidential diplomatic files.

River let herself be led out of the room and tried not

to let her anger grow. She tried not to imagine the worst in the stupid dragon she was somehow supposed to romance or what she would do if she had ten minutes to really take her anger out on Seth for asking her to do such a thing.

Seth and Ash headed for their meeting and she went outside. The school had just gotten out and the children were running around like animals near the play area. Watching their antics washed away some of her anger, especially as a little girl chased one of the boys until he was forced to climb some of the equipment to get away from her.

"River! River!" a small, high-pitched voice called as she turned to head home.

She looked down and saw a short blonde curly head that only came up to her stomach. The head tipped back to reveal Carli, one of the students who should have been playing. "Hey, little one." She ruffled Carli's hair gently. She'd watched the child when Carli was just a baby as a favor to Carli's parents who'd been working all hours on a project. Now she felt like an honorary aunt to the girl. "You should be playing."

"Mama said you're going away soon." It might have been a sad sentence if not for the bright smile on the girl's face. "You're gonna go meet important people and help the planet."

In the face of Carli's smile, she couldn't tell the girl that her job was apparently to smile and flirt. And

Carli's enthusiasm went some way to reigniting her own.

Screw Seth. Maybe he thought she was only good for seducing a dragon. She'd show him. She was going to be the best diplomat out of the lot of them, and this trip was going to be the first of many. Seth would eat his words when they were done. She'd make him.

But Carli didn't need to know that. River smiled and hugged Carli to her side. "Yeah," she said. "I am."

CHAPTER
THREE

"WAS THERE SOMETHING YOU NEEDED, Lord Storm?" Lore, the head diplomat asked as Storm loitered in the entrance to the temporary office that had been set up on their ship.

Storm tried to hide his scowl. Lore was one of the most respected peacetime diplomats on Vemion and anyone else would think it an honor to work under him. Certainly the other dragons on this mission, Echo, Rush, and Night were of that opinion.

Storm felt like a useless piece of furniture. Something decorative that went in the middle of the room and couldn't be sat on, leaned against, or used as a table. Purely decorative and a waste of space.

"No." Storm backed out of the door and let it slide closed before he was forced into conversation.

That was the story of the entire last month. The

stupid matchmaker had gotten into his head. The morning after their ill-fated meeting, he'd been given his marching orders by the king. He was on a diplomatic mission to speak with a small human planet about opening up a trade route. His presence was a sign of good will.

He wished he'd told the king to shove off.

But he was pretty sure that was treason. Even when the king was his uncle.

Now Shade's prediction was in his head: he'd meet his mate when he followed the king's order. Except he didn't want to meet his mate. The only female dragon on the mission was Echo, and while she was beautiful and kind, he felt nothing for her. He couldn't even call her his friend.

A smart dragon would try to get to know her and determine if she could be his destiny.

Instead Storm kept his distance. He didn't need some stupid destiny getting in the way of his life. He was good. Fine. Perfectly happy.

His mother's threat may have been hanging over his head, but he wouldn't dance to her tune simply because she played the music.

He stalked through the narrow hallways of the ship in a foul mood. They were an hour or so off from making landfall in the Dominion on a small planet with space that had been rented to act as a neutral location. Neither the humans nor the dragons had treaties with the Dominion, and neither planet was at war with them. Conveniently, the edge of the Dominion lay right between their two territories which made the meeting place seem like fate.

Fate could find someone else to screw with.

All Storm had to do was get through this mission, not completely screw it up, and go home without a mate. He'd left the planet dozens of times and never found his mate, why should this time be any different?

Why are you fighting this so hard? A voice in his head that sounded an awful lot like Drake's asked.

But his brother wasn't with him, and there was no need to answer phantom brothers.

This wasn't where Storm wanted to be. Even if he'd wanted his mate. Which he didn't. His mother was the diplomat. Her work had taken her halfway across the galaxy and she'd been gone for giant portions of his childhood. Her work was important, the kind that kept Vemion safe and prosperous.

But it left her sons alone.

Storm was a man now. Why was he dwelling on his mother's neglect when it had been decades since it mattered? All that mattered now was making sure she continued *not* running his life.

"You're smoking." His only friend on the mission, Night, appeared around one of the tight corners of the ship and stopped when he saw Storm.

"I'm fine," Storm muttered. He and Night had gone

to school together as boys, and then the Academy as young men. They'd fallen out of touch in recent years, but if there was one good thing about this mission, it was seeing his friend again.

Night gave an exaggerated cough. "Did Rush say something? I can't imagine Lore making anyone angry."

"Everything is fine," Storm insisted. He leaned against the wall, crossed his arms, and took a few deep breaths, pulling his smoke back inside of himself. He had to get better control, he was letting his emotions rule him like he was still a dragonling.

Night raised an eyebrow and pursed his lips. "Right." He leaned back and waited for Storm to talk, but when Storm kept his mouth clamped shut, Night huffed out a laugh and shook his head. "If we need anyone who won't break under torture, you'll be my first candidate." He paused, but Storm still kept his mouth shut. "Rumor has it you spoke with the Royal Matchmaker."

Storm groaned. So much for not breaking under torture. "No. Don't do this. I beg of you."

"If you didn't want rumors swirling, you shouldn't have met with her so openly in a tavern. My mother heard it from three different people before sunrise." Night was grinning now. "Is the mighty Storm ready to find his bride?"

"The only suitable woman on this journey is Echo.

Do you want me to try?" He raised his eyebrows at Night in challenge.

And his friend's face descended into darkness. Then it abruptly cleared. "If Echo wants to be your lady bride, that is her choice."

It was on the tip of Storm's tongue to tease his friend. He'd seen the looks that Night sent Echo's way, and heard how the man became tongue tied whenever he tried to talk to her about anything except the mission. If he'd truly been considering Echo as a bride, he would have had to consider Night's feelings. He didn't want to swoop in and steal his friend's woman before Night even had a chance.

But if Storm truly wanted a woman, he wouldn't fall over his own tongue to talk to her.

"I'm not here for Echo," he said, giving Night a reprieve. "The matchmaker spoke nonsense. I'm on this mission because my uncle commanded me, no other reason. And I shall return home just as unmated as I left."

That made Night stand up straighter. "You're searching for your mate?"

"I'm *not*. And if I were, wouldn't I be wiser to stay home where most of the dragons live? It's hard to find a mate on another planet."

"Your cousins did," Night pointed out. "Humans, even. Perhaps your mate will be among those we're meeting."

"Don't even mention it. Please." Storm shuddered to think about it. While he didn't want to dance to his mother's tune, he didn't want to antagonize her either. And bringing home a human mate would be tantamount to a declaration of war. Not only would he *not* be her heir, he'd be expelled from the family completely.

The ship jolted and Echo's voice came over the loudspeaker. "Prepare for landing. We are approaching our destination."

That ended any conversation. Night continued down the hall to wherever he meant to go while Storm found a nearby seat and strapped in. The descent was bumpy, but fast, and in a matter of minutes they were landing at their destination.

Storm stayed buckled in his seat for several moments, hands hovering over his restraints. His talk with Night put him back in mind of the matchmaker and the nonsense she'd spoken.

What if he met his mate out there? What if she was waiting for him?

He didn't need the complication that would bring. He was happy on his own. Truly. And with that firmly in mind, he unbuckled and headed for the exit. He could use some fresh air.

The space they'd rented was an entire sector of this Dominion planet. There were no residents around for miles and miles, though the nearest city was only about seventy kilometers away. They had the privacy they needed to conduct their business, but could call for assistance if it was necessary.

Storm breathed in deep and savored the fresh air after days spent on the ship. The air filtration system was as fine as could be had in all of Vemion, but nothing beat the air on a planet full of trees and greenery.

Another ship was parked in the landing area. The humans were already here. And a quick glance saw that they were loitering on the edge of the field.

Storm gave them a look. He'd been given a dossier with information about each of them, but he'd ignored it, as if it would make the job less real. He counted five heads, but could only make out three figures, given the way they were huddled.

The human diplomats looked his way, and he realized he was the first off the ship. Probably some breach of custom. He really didn't care.

Then the humans stepped aside and the woman in their group stepped forward. She had long blonde hair that fell down over her shoulders in waves. Her skin was kissed by the sun of her planet, her lips wide with a small smile tugging them to one side. If he was closer, he might have seen what her eyes looked like.

He needed to see. Needed to *know*.

That desire had him stepping down the ramp, but sanity stopped him before he did something foolish.

And a moment later he was joined by his fellow diplomats, and Lore hurried forward to do the introduction.

But Storm couldn't keep his eyes off the woman. And before the day was done, he was going to know her name.

"THAT'S HIM." Seth nudged River's shoulder, as if she needed an extra reminder that she was meant to get to know Lord Storm.

She and her fellow diplomats were huddled on the edge of the landing area and had been waiting for nearly an hour for the dragons to show up. The facilitators provided by the facility they were using had insisted that they could not be allowed inside until all parties appeared.

And now the dragons were here.

Seth and Ash stepped aside to let her get her first look at Lord Storm. And when she did, she almost swallowed her tongue.

The picture didn't do him justice.

He stood like a hero from some ancient statue and surveyed the area around him like he owned it. Maybe that was just how lords were. River wouldn't know. They didn't have any back home. His jaw was covered in a light peppering of dark hair that gave him a rakish look and framed lips that were almost too red, even from across a field. His eyes looked dark, but she couldn't be sure of their color, and when his fellow dragons stepped out onto the ramp with him, she saw he had a handful of centimeters on all of them.

She liked a tall man.

Not that she should be caring.

But for a moment, Seth's insinuating suggestion didn't seem so bad. Would it be so bad to seduce a man who looked like *that?*

Of course, he wasn't a man. And even if he was, a man like that wouldn't bother to give her the time of day.

And even if he would, it didn't matter. Seth's idea was still ringing in her head and she refused on principle to entertain it. She was just as much a diplomat as the others in her group, even if she was new to it. And she wouldn't begin her career with an attempted seduction.

No matter how hot her target was.

It was too bad. She'd never slept with a dragon before, and she probably wouldn't get another chance.

River deliberately turned away from him, angling so she could take in the view around them. Considering how gorgeous this little slice of the Dominion was, the fact that she had to drag her eyes away from Lord Storm said something.

Hills rolled all around them, and their meeting place sat in a valley. Those hills were covered with greenery and moss, and a strange mist hung in the air all around them. This was a place that felt like it had history and a bit of sorrow, though she couldn't say why that occurred to her.

Beyond the hills and over them were thick green trees that muffled the sounds from all around, giving them the illusion that they were the only people on the planet. River knew it was false; she'd seen the city they flew over on the way to their landing spot. But it might as well have been on another planet.

It was a good place for an ambush.

That sent a shiver up her spine and she tried to push the thought away. This was neutral territory. Neither her party nor the dragons had any problems with the Dominion, and the Domini were a proud and militant people. They'd ensure no one was hurt during this meeting.

Still, the hills would be an excellent hiding place. Maybe that was their history. Maybe sometime long before this planet joined the Dominion or ventured into the stars, ancient raiders had laid in wait for unwary travelers to venture through.

Looking at the hills was even more of a distraction than looking at the newcomers.

"What?" Seth didn't yell, but his voice was right on the edge of anger. "That is unacceptable."

She hadn't been paying attention, but now she turned her focus towards the group. One of the Domini facilitators who would be with them throughout the duration of this summit was trying to placate the human leader. "I apologize, sir. I had hoped the power issues in the luncheon room would be fixed by the time the delegation from Vemion arrived, but the electrician says he needs a little more time. Please allow us another hour to repair things. If the room is not ready by then, we shall set up your luncheon at an alternate location."

Oh. Well. That was… simple. And Seth didn't have any room to truly get angry, but she could see it simmering within him. The trip had been long enough and they'd all been on top of each other in the days it took to get here. A meal would be more than welcome.

The air beside her moved, and suddenly River felt a *presence* right in her space. Heat radiated off of him, and when she glanced back, she was unsurprised to find Lord Storm standing right there.

It was instinct to smile politely at him. She wanted to say something, but couldn't find her tongue. Besides, she was pretty sure that was a breach of protocol. Seth was supposed to make introductions for the humans while the dragon leader did the same for his party. Then they were meant to get to know each other a little at the introductory luncheon. Negotiations didn't start until tomorrow.

Lord Storm cleared his throat and she glanced at him again, but he didn't say anything.

Okay, so he was following the rules.

Seth argued with the facilitator for a few more minutes, but he couldn't magically fix an electrical problem.

One of the dragons stepped forward before Seth could do something unforgivable, like wring the facilitator's neck.

"Greetings all, my name is Lore and I am glad to meet you. Please, let me do our introductions. And once things are ready, we may proceed to lunch. I do believe we'll have time beforehand to find our sleeping quarters, so this will work out well." He had the kind of calming voice she expected from grandparents, or really good teachers, though he didn't look old enough to be a grandparent.

River gave him all of her attention, but she couldn't ignore the dragon burning himself into her consciousness right beside her. She had to, though, before she did something embarrassing, like throw him down on the ground and demand that he take her now.

She was here to do a job. She'd just keep her distance from the sexy dragon and all would be well.

CHAPTER
FIVE

TWO DAYS into this stupid endeavor and Storm couldn't be more frustrated. The moment he'd stepped off the ship there'd been a glimmer of hope when he spotted the gorgeous River. He was trying to ignore the fact that his tongue had tied itself in knots when he tried to speak to her.

It wouldn't happen again.

The electrical issue in the luncheon room had been fixed and he'd hoped he would manage to sidle up beside her then. But she'd ensconced herself with another human and they'd both monopolized Rush. He'd been forced to sit with the boorish human leader and hold his tongue while the man attempted to flatter him.

Storm only had a week, perhaps two if things stretched out, to get closer to River, and something inside of him demanded that he do it. He wasn't thinking about the matchmaker at all when it came to River. She was a human, she wouldn't be his mate. The chances were so slim he didn't have to worry.

But attraction like this came fast and burned hot, Storm knew. He wanted to give it a chance before he flew away, never to see the beautiful River again.

So why was she hiding from him?

Perhaps he was being a bit dramatic, but he could do that in the privacy of his own mind. As long as Night didn't see him losing his mind for a woman, he'd be safe. He'd never survive the teasing his old friend would give him.

But it would be worth it for one evening with River in his bed.

He was meant to be heading to dinner, but had lost track of time and was now late. He knew he shouldn't be dawdling in the hallways and hoping that River appeared. She was likely already seated and hadn't even noticed he was gone.

Lore would notice. He might even say something. Storm wasn't exactly a prodigy at diplomacy, though he hadn't screwed anything major up yet. Though doing so would almost certainly mean he never had to go on one of these missions again, he was too proud to do it intentionally. And clearly this meeting was important to the king. He didn't want to let his uncle down.

"You twisted piece of useless metal. I'll send you to the trash heap if you don't open."

River's voice was a siren song, pulling him helplessly down the corridor that housed the rooms the humans were staying in. Technically he wasn't supposed to go there, but she sounded like she needed help.

And then she let out a stream of curses that had him raising his eyebrows. He hadn't heard some of those words since the Academy.

She stood in front of the door to her quarters and had her hand on the handle, squeezing it for all she was worth. She pressed her shoulder against it and pushed, but the doors were solid and he knew it wouldn't budge.

River pulled back and smacked the metal, then pulled her hand away and shook it, wincing in pain.

"Is all well?" Storm asked. He made himself stay several steps away, just in case she got the wrong idea. They were alone in the residential corridor and both of their parties were on the far side of the building in the dining room. He didn't want her to see him as a threat.

River slumped against the door. "My door isn't accepting my code." Then her eyes got big and her face lit up. "You're a dragon, right? Can you burn it down for me?"

His chest puffed up a little and if he had just a little less sense he might have tried. He wanted her to see just how big his flame could get. Instead, he took one step closer. "May I?"

"Not for real!" Her eyes widened even further and she put her body in front of the door, as if she could somehow block his flame.

Storm laughed. "No, not that. There's a trick to opening the doors. Mine acted up earlier."

It had been a nuisance at the time, but now he would gladly take a hundred faulty doors if it gave him an excuse to talk to River.

"Oh." She shook her head a little and huffed a laugh. "Of course. Sure. Tell me when to put my code in." Her hand hovered over the keypad.

Storm grabbed the doorknob and twisted it as much as he could, even though it was still locked. He got about an eighth of a turn. Then he pushed down on the handle and nodded at her. "Go for it."

She punched in her code and the light on the sensor turned green. He heard the lock disengage and he pushed with all his might.

The door opened.

"Yes!" She pumped her fist. "You're a miracle worker." She stepped closer until they were almost touching and he could smell the faint floral scent of her soap. "Thank you."

He was so caught up in her presence that he didn't hear the footsteps coming towards them until Seth's voice interrupted them. "Ah, there you two are. Skipping dinner, eh?" There was something in his congenial tone that Storm didn't like, an insinuation that shouldn't be there.

River's face shut down, her expression completely blank. She took a step back. "My door was malfunctioning. Lord Storm assisted me. Thank you, your lordship." She turned to Seth. "I'll be along to dinner shortly." Then she slipped into her room and left the two of them alone in the hall.

But there was only one human Storm wanted to be near, and he had to let her know there was no need to stand on ceremony. He wouldn't want her calling him *your lordship* when she was in his bed.

If he could find a way to get her there.

And he didn't want Seth asking questions about why he was in the human's residential corridor.

So Storm retreated. But this wasn't over. He was going to find River, and he was going to enjoy every minute he had of her. She might just make this excursion bearable.

CHAPTER
SIX

RIVER HATED TO ADMIT IT, but diplomacy was kind of boring.

The humans were broadly in agreement about opening up trade and tourism between their two planets. Now they were just hammering out the finer details. There were a surprising number of spreadsheets involved.

And she felt useless. She'd sat at the table and listened, but had nothing to add to the discussions. It was another unwelcome reminder of why Seth had let her come along on this mission. And with everything going so well, she had no way to distinguish herself, no way to prove she belonged here.

Okay, now she was just being childish. She couldn't hope the mission went poorly just so she could show up and save the day. That thought might have actually bordered on treason. But she still wanted to matter.

Thankfully they were on a break for now. And the second it was called, she'd been out of the building and on the nice walking path that led deeper into the valley. She needed the time alone, and this area was so gorgeous it deserved to be appreciated.

A strange sound overhead caught her attention and she looked up, but there was nothing there. Nothing at all until the shadow of a dragon swooped over her and spun around before letting out a burst of fire that made her gasp.

River almost clapped at the performance, but stopped herself when she realized it might be rude. And though she couldn't help the negotiations, she could certainly hurt them by wounding a dragon's pride.

The dragon kept flying and she watched him go, her heart pounding a little fast, both from the excitement of his display, and with a bit of longing. What would it be like to be up in the air like that? She couldn't imagine that kind of freedom.

It was the first time she'd seen a dragon transformed in person. She'd seen videos, but those didn't really capture the experience, not correctly. For one thing, that dragon was *huge*. He probably couldn't fit on the ship they'd flown on in that form. A part of her thought that he looked like an ancient monster.

But she wanted to get closer.

Without much thought, River walked in the same direction he'd flown, hoping to get a better look. Obviously the dragon could cover a ton more distance than she could, but that didn't stop her. And it wasn't like she had any great need to get back to the meetings. They probably wouldn't even notice if she was gone.

She lost track of time on her walk, but her legs were aching and she was far enough away that she could no longer see a hint of the compound where they were staying. The sun was starting to hang low in the sky, a hint that she should turn back before it got dark and hiking got dangerous.

She hadn't meant to walk so far.

And she hadn't seen the dragon again.

Which one was it? The dossiers she had on each of the dragons gave information about their achievements and all available public records, but they said little about their dragon forms. All she knew was that the dragon couldn't be Night because Night was meant to be an inky black with a spattering of white spots that looked like stars.

His dragon form was apparently quite famous among his people.

Some part of her hoped it was Storm. She hoped she'd turn a corner and find him lounging on the ground where he'd smile at her and offer her a ride.

Of some kind.

But since she was still determined to keep her distance, that moment by her room notwithstanding, the saner part of her had to hope it *wasn't* Storm—Lord Storm—out for a flight. She had to remember that title. People with titles probably got testy when you forgot them.

She heard the sound again, and this time she whipped around quickly enough to see the dragon approaching her. It was flying high and she stood still to take in the majesty of its flight.

Or that was the plan.

Then the dragon dove straight for her.

She scurried back, but she was at the foot of one of the valley's many hills and tripped over something, half falling, half leaning on the surprisingly steep incline.

Strangely, she thought she heard masculine laughter echoing in her head.

"That's not very funny!" she yelled at the dragon as she got to her feet and glared at where he circled above her.

If anything, the laughter grew louder.

Okay, she was clearly going crazy.

I've seen turkeys scarier than you, she thought grouchily at the hovering beast.

In the sky, the dragon stuttered and suddenly dropped a dozen feet before he wildly beat his wings to regain his altitude. After a moment he glided down, and by the time he landed he was in his human form, wearing a dark uniform that looked a little militaristic.

The transformation had happened so fast that River hadn't realized it was happening until it was over.

"Are you okay?" she asked, once her mind caught up to the fact that Storm—Lord Storm—was striding toward her like some sort of warrior of old.

His gaze was intense, and it was like he held her in a tractor beam. She couldn't look away, couldn't move. Couldn't do anything until he was right on her and close enough to touch.

To kiss.

"Did you—"

Whatever question he was asking was cut off by a loud bang in the distance followed by an even louder boom.

Both coming from the diplomatic compound.

They both took off running.

CHAPTER
SEVEN

BESIDE HIM, River was lagging as they got close to the compound. Part of Storm wanted to take off ahead and scout, the other part wouldn't dare let his mate out of his sight.

Mate?

Maybe.

He could have sworn that her voice echoed in his head during his flight. Only a mate could have communicated with him telepathically.

But there was also a chance he'd imagined it.

"Get down!" River tugged on his arm and dragged him behind a small collection of bushes that delineated the edge of the compound's tended grounds and the wild valley beyond. They could just see the edge of the residential building and the lots where their ships were parked. If he moved to the other edge of the bushes, he'd make out the building where they'd been meeting.

He didn't see a crater, though the explosion had sounded intense.

Was this a double cross by the humans? As soon as he considered it, he threw the thought away. What purpose would it serve? There had never been any threat of violence between their two planets, and this mission was about tourism.

And though his mind went directly to thinking there was an attack, he couldn't guarantee it. The compound had been riddled with tiny mishaps the entire time they'd been there. That blast could have been from faulty wiring.

But if it was, why didn't he see anyone?

"Are your people attacking us?" There was a waver in River's voice and her shoulders were set as if she was ready to launch an attack of her own. "*Why?*"

"Not us, no reason to do it." He looked closer at the compound and cursed when he got to the field where three ships were parked.

There should have only been two.

He studied the small craft. Domini make, he was almost certain. Short haul, limited ability to break atmo, mostly used for flying on the planet. And depending on the seating arrangements, it could probably hold fifty people.

If there were fifty Domini soldiers in the compound, they were dead.

The ramp of the ship was down and two Dominis walked down, both wearing dark armor with no identification badges that Storm could make out.

Mercs.

He pulled River back, keeping low but not stopping until they made it to a small copse of trees at the foot of one of the hills.

"Shouldn't we be going to help?" she asked once he finally stopped. She looked back over her shoulder, but they were too far away to see much.

She was brave, this human. Any man would be proud to have her as his mate.

And Storm would be a fool not to claim her. If she was his.

He wanted to laugh at himself, and maybe he would have if the situation wasn't so dire. He'd been determined to spite his mother and the matchmaker. Yet here he was in the moment where he might have found his mate, and he couldn't even consider walking away.

"St—Lord Storm?" River prompted.

"Just Storm, please. No formality between us." His title could be a weapon when he used it cruelly, and he'd never do that to her. "There was a Dominion craft parked beside our two ships. I spotted two people, possibly mercs. I didn't see any damage to the buildings, but from that angle we only saw a sliver of the buildings. Whatever damage there is could be contained to the north side."

"What do you think those sounds were?" Her voice quavered for a moment but she closed her eyes and took a deep breath. When she opened them, she was as steady as steel.

Yes, anyone would be proud to have her as his mate.

Storm had to think of the mission first, though. At least his mate—his potential mate—wasn't in mercenary clutches. And he'd make sure it stayed that way. Somehow.

"Probably some sort of explosive to blast through a fortified door. The compound does have some rudimentary defenses. They're all automated. And they mostly exist on the assumption that strife will come from parties already inside the building. The best case scenario is that our two parties have barricaded themselves in a room and managed to call for help. The fact that no help was here when we arrived suggests that isn't the case." It had taken more than an hour to cover the distance they'd both traveled throughout the day. He could have flown faster, but they would have spotted him coming from several kilometers away.

"Are they dead?" she asked.

He wanted to reassure her, but he couldn't lie. "I

don't know. But if this was a hit, it would be quick. Little reason to linger."

"Unless they wanted to kill us too."

He'd been trying not to say that part, but he nodded. If they had the expertise to quickly breach the compound, these mercenaries likely had enough information to know how many diplomats to expect. A simple headcount would reveal they were missing.

"You're a dragon, can't you go and fight them?" She scrunched up her hands like she had claws and jerked them in front of her face.

His warrior form could take a lot of damage. His sky form even more. But there were drawbacks. "I'm not charging in without knowing how many mercs are in there. And I'm not leaving you vulnerable. Do you have your comm? We need backup."

She patted her pocket and groaned. "Damn it. I must have left it in my quarters. What about you?"

"No. While the shift can accommodate clothes, sometimes it wreaks havoc on electronics. I left mine behind to be safe." A foolish move. Most of the time a communicator survived just fine. But when things went wrong, whatever magic allowed him to shift and swallowed up his comms made him *itch*. It was unpleasant. "At least I'm clothed. Some legends claim we must be fully nude to take our other forms."

Her eyes flicked up and down. "Yeah. That would be a real shame." Then she jerked her gaze away from him. "Okay, we need a plan. Can you fly to the city for help? I can hunker down in the woods. I was a wilderness camper as a kid. I'll be safe enough."

"I'm not leaving you alone out here." Before they could argue any further, he heard a noise, and they both clamped their mouths shut.

Storm looked down the path towards the compound and cursed. The area where they'd been standing by the bushes was now occupied by a large security robot. Its head swiveled back and forth, scanning for something.

Scanning for them.

He grabbed River's hand and pulled her deeper into the valley. There was no telling what exactly that bot could scan for or what its range was, but he wanted safely out of it.

"It's several hours flight by wing to the city," he said as they marched. He wanted over the hill and beyond it, but the higher ground could expose them. They'd have to stay at the base of the hills and go around what landmarks they could until they were well away from the compound.

Maybe River's wilderness skills would come in handy.

"And I'd need to get far enough away that they couldn't see my take off. It would leave you too exposed here. I won't lead them to you. I'd offer to let you ride me out of here, but it's far too cold in the clouds." She was wearing a short sleeved top and pants that hugged her hips in a way that gave him ideas. The weather on the ground was pleasant enough for light clothes. She'd freeze in the air without a jacket.

"Okay, so we can't call for help. We can't go into the building. We can't fight the bad guys, and you won't go for help. We need to do *something* or they're going to find us before long." She squeezed her eyes shut and clutched at her head. "Let me think."

They were far away enough that he felt safe pausing for the moment. He let River do her thing.

"There's supposed to be a groundskeepers' cabin on the other side of the valley. I remember the facilitator mentioning it when I asked him about the upkeep here. He assured me that the groundskeepers didn't stay near the compound when meetings were in session. So maybe the cabin's empty. And maybe there's a comm. Or a vehicle. I'm not sure exactly where it is, but the valley path isn't exactly complicated. What do you say?"

It was a lot of maybes. And they didn't know whether or not the facilitators were involved in the treachery.

But they didn't have options.

"Let's go."

CHAPTER
EIGHT

NIGHT HAD FULLY FALLEN by the time they made it to the groundskeepers' cabin and River wanted to sob in relief. Her feet were killing her, every muscle in her body was stiff, and she was wound so tight she feared she might shatter.

What had started as a pleasant walk quickly turned into a nightmare as surveillance drones started scanning the valley.

Storm had an uncanny penchant for sensing them, but there had been more than one close call. She especially hated the time Storm had tackled her to the ground and she'd landed on a rock the size of a fist. She'd have bruises for days.

But she refused to complain. He didn't need a weakling at his side. And though she'd so bravely told him about her wilderness training, now that she'd seen the drones and they'd driven home the threat, she didn't want to be alone.

Whoever those bad guys were back at the compound would find her before she could even try to evade them. She didn't want to be a hostage.

Or worse.

The cabin was as dark as the night outside, barely an outline in the pale moonlight. But it was the promise of shelter, and possibly safety.

She hoped.

If the mercenaries found them here, she wasn't sure she had any more energy to run.

The front door was mercifully unlocked, and once they stepped inside, the place smelled stale, as if no one had been there for at least a few days, perhaps weeks. She reached for the light switch, but somehow Storm saw her and clamped his hand over hers.

"Not yet," he warned. "We don't want to become a beacon."

Right. Lights at night weren't good when you were trying to hide.

But after a moment, light bloomed in his hands and she wondered if he had a match or a lighter before she remembered he was a dragon. He *was* a match.

She couldn't stop staring at the flame in his hands and she understood moths a little better. There was something irresistible about it, some siren call that made her want to reach out and take some of the fire for herself.

Which was crazy. She didn't want to get burned.

The flame hovered in Storm's hand for a second. "Let me try something," he said cautiously. "Do you trust me?"

That was a hell of a question. What was she supposed to say to the man who controlled their only light source? "Um, sure. I guess."

A resounding and unequivocal yes might have been the wiser mood, but River was a terrible liar.

"Hold your hand out. If it hurts, if it's even a bit too warm, tell me." He brought the hand holding his flame right beside hers. "Come on."

"You've gotta be crazy. I can't hold fire!" Her fingers curled into fists at the thought. There had to be a flashlight around here somewhere.

"I think this will work," he insisted. "I will pull the flame back immediately if it doesn't. I promise."

She had to be crazy to consider this. He was a dragon. Maybe he didn't understand just how flammable humans could be. But he sounded confident. So maybe there was some kind of dragon trick that would allow her to do this.

The day was already unbelievable enough. What was one more thing?

She flattened her palm beside his. "Do it before I change my mind."

He tipped the fire over onto her outstretched hand and River braced herself, sure she'd be scalded at any moment. Instead, all she felt was the faintest tickle. She held perfectly still and stared at the flame until dark circles danced in her eyes and she was forced to blink and look away.

"Holy crap." She was afraid to move her hand, as if that might break the spell.

Storm let out a long breath of his own. "You—" He cut himself off and took a step back, summoning another ball of fire for himself. "You're—you can move," he said. "You should be able to control that flame on your own. If you accidentally extinguish it, I'll make you a new one. Just be careful while we look around. Let's see if we can cover up the windows. Then we can see about electric lights."

There was something in his voice that she couldn't decipher, something that sounded important. Maybe if she could see him properly, if the room was illuminated by more than essentially two large candles, she could get an idea of what he wasn't saying.

But she was holding magical fire in the palm of her hand and it was too cool to contemplate.

"Is this a dragon trick?" she asked. "I didn't know you could do this. How?"

"We need to get these windows covered," he repeated.

Well. Alright then. Apparently giving someone else

the ability to touch fire without being burned was just an everyday thing in dragon land and he couldn't even spend a second explaining.

River moved carefully, and her body protested every movement. The fire wasn't spectacular enough to make her forget her aches and pains, apparently. But it didn't take long for her to find a switch that controlled the shutters on the windows. She winced as metal clanked, but in a matter of seconds, every window was covered by a storm shutter and no light would leak outside.

Storm flipped the light switch and River winced at the sudden brightness. But she still had the fire in her palm and she didn't want to let go of it. She was tempted to try some tricks, to see if she could pass it from hand to hand or change the size of the flame, but she worried she might set something ablaze.

Or that she'd look like a fool in front of Storm.

She closed her fist and the fire disappeared.

Storm was staring at her and breathing as hard as if he'd just run a long distance race. If another man looked at her like that, she might think he had wicked thoughts running through his mind.

But a dragon lord was so far out of her league she couldn't even contemplate it.

River took in the cottage around them. It was cozy, with a bed tucked in one corner, a small kitchen and eating area on the other side, and a quarter of the room dedicated to an entertainment station with a couch barely big enough to fit two people. She spotted a bathroom through an open door.

It wasn't much, but it beat camping where the surveillance drones could find them.

"Do you see a communicator?" Storm asked. He was down on his hands and knees, looking under the bed.

She jolted as she remembered she was supposed to be looking. "Not yet." She dedicated herself to the task, but no matter how hard she looked, she didn't see one.

"I'll be right back," Storm said, and he was out the front door before she could ask what he meant by that. Two minutes later, he was inside and grimacing. "There's a small electric riding cart that looks like it can cover the grounds but no further. I didn't see a vehicle capable of taking us to the city."

Damn it.

She waited for Storm to suggest that he could fly to the city now that she was safe in the cabin. It made a certain kind of sense. If the mercenaries didn't know the cabin was there, they wouldn't search it. And as long as they kept the windows covered, even if they found it, they might assume it was vacant.

But River didn't suggest that he should go. She didn't want to be alone, didn't want to risk being discovered. She'd been pushing away fear as best she could for the last several hours, but now her limbs were threatening to shake.

If she was alone, she'd dissolve into a puddle of tears and terror, and she wasn't sure she'd recover.

She shuffled across the room, intending to take a seat on the couch. There was only one bed and Storm was bigger than her. He should take it. And she really didn't want to get into an argument about that.

"Is something wrong?" the dragon asked. "Why are you limping?"

She eased herself down onto the couch with a groan. "You tackled me right into a nasty rock and we walked at least a dozen kilometers. I'm tired, that's all." She curled up onto her side and tried not to imagine how much her body was going to hurt in the morning from sleeping in this position.

"You know, I've been told I give a very decent massage. Can I help you? As payback for tackling you?" He was still standing near the door, and he looked like an invitation to sin.

River should probably say no. This was the weirdest, most harrowing day of her life. She might actually go mad if it ended with her being rubbed down by a dragon lord.

But when would she ever get the chance?

"Okay."

He smiled like she'd done him a favor. "You should lay on the bed for this. It'll be easier."

She didn't want to move. Already she could feel her muscles freezing into place, but she forced herself up and to make the four steps to the bed. "How do you want me?"

Was it her imagination or did Storm groan?

"On your stomach. And, if you're comfortable, may I put my hands under your shirt? I can warm my palms with my flame and it will feel very good skin to skin." He sounded professional, like he had some kind of second life as a dragon masseuse.

And it made her bold. Or maybe that was the exhaustion. River turned around to face the wall and peeled off her shirt, tossing it to the ground before she lay flat on the bed. She lay there alone for several moments and she didn't hear Storm move.

Then he was right over her, his hands warm on her back as his palms pressed against her tight skin and worked at relaxing the muscles underneath. He was right. His palms were warm enough to sit right on the edge between amazing and uncomfortable, and he pressed against her hard, not trying to treat her like some delicate rose who would crumple with the slightest pressure.

A moan escaped, and River felt so good she couldn't care that it sounded like he was touching her somewhere else entirely.

"Do you like that?" His voice was rough and low, a whisper and a promise she wanted to hold close.

She moaned again, meaning to make it a yes and failing.

This was going to stay with her for the rest of forever, she was sure. The dragon lord lovingly running his hands along her back like he was made to make her feel good. No one back home would believe her and she didn't care. This was a memory just for her.

She didn't realize she was about to fall asleep, but she slipped into unconsciousness while reveling in the feel of Storm's hands.

CHAPTER
NINE

A BETTER MAN would have curled up on the couch and let River take the bed alone.

Storm was only so strong. And the bed was just big enough for the two of them if he slept on his side. He couldn't resist, especially when it gave him the perfect view of River.

Once she'd slipped into sleep he'd covered her with a blanket, even though it seemed a crime to hide her no doubt luscious breasts. But he hadn't looked. It had taken a heroic amount of willpower, but he'd averted his gaze. She'd allowed him to touch her naked back, but hadn't invited him to view her naked front.

In sleep, her face had lost its tension and she looked a little younger. He hoped that he'd taken away enough of her pain that the morning wouldn't be torture. He didn't want his mate to suffer.

He let out an unsteady breath. It had been a risk, giving her that ball of flame. If she weren't his, it would have singed her hands or worse if he didn't extinguish it quickly enough. But she'd spoken in his head while he was in his dragon form. He'd been nearly sure.

And now he was certain.

River was his fated mate. A human. A gorgeous human who sent his mind into dark and dirty places and made him want to promise her the stars.

Yet he hadn't said a word about it to her, despite the fact that she'd given him an opening by asking. But bringing it up felt like leading them into even more shaky territory. There were mercenaries at the compound, they didn't have a way to call for help, and he wasn't leaving her alone and vulnerable for the hours it would take for him to go for help.

Adding mating on top of all of that might just be enough to send her running. And he couldn't fight two wars at once.

No. It was best to keep that to himself for now. He could woo her without the added pressure of fate pressing down on them. And once they were safe, he could reveal all. He wasn't hiding the truth, he reasoned, simply delaying it.

But his mate was not his biggest worry. He cursed himself for leaving both his communicator and his rescue beacon in his quarters. The beacon was an emergency device that all members of the royal family were supposed to carry with them whenever they were off planet. It had always seemed like overkill to Storm. The king might be his uncle, but he wouldn't let him rule his life.

And now the beacon was sitting silently in his belongings, completely useless.

He couldn't summon help from home, and they couldn't get a message out to the city in the hopes that help would come from the Dominion.

Of course, there was always the possibility that the Dominion was responsible for this attack. They could be hiding behind mercenaries to obscure their involvement. But Storm didn't think they were. He hoped they weren't. They wouldn't survive if the entire planet was about to turn against them.

And he had just found his mate. Survival was a must.

He eventually drifted off to sleep and woke some hours later to find his arm slung over River and hear her stomach growling.

She woke and froze as she realized their positions. But she didn't try to push his arm away. "Um… good morning?"

Storm pulled away and shimmied off the bed as if nothing unusual had happened. He couldn't be held responsible for an unconscious cuddle, but he didn't want to make his mate uncomfortable. And she needed food.

"Good morning," he said. Nights were short on this planet, so he was certain the sun was up, even if he couldn't tell beyond the shutters covering the windows. "How are you feeling? Your muscles, I mean?" He sounded like an eager schoolboy, and he was tripping over his own tongue trying to make River feel well.

She sat up slowly and then scrambled to clutch the blanket to her chest as she realized she was topless. Her cheeks flamed red. "I'm fine. Maybe just a little sore." Her eyes darted around the room until they snagged on her shirt, which was lying on the ground. "Could you turn around, please?" Her voice went up an entire octave as she asked.

Storm did better than that. He turned and went into the kitchen while she dressed, digging through cupboards to find anything they could eat. There were a few cans of vegetables in one cupboard and a box of meal bars in another. Storm recognized the brand on the packaging and shuddered. The meal bars would taste like soggy cardboard.

But at least they'd sate hunger. It was better than starving.

Barely.

He put the canned vegetables back. They might

taste better than the meal bars, but they'd require prep, and he didn't want to waste time.

When he turned around, two meal bars in hand, River was fully dressed and the blankets had been laid over the bed. It didn't look as if anyone had slept in it.

"I don't suppose a communicator magically appeared in the night?" she asked.

He handed over a meal bar. "Afraid not."

She unwrapped it and took a big bite and made a face when the taste hit her. But she kept eating. She must have been very hungry. He ate slower, bracing against every bite. It was possible the taste actually got worse the more he ate. Maybe his mate had the right idea. He shoved the last third of the bar in his mouth and chewed quickly, nearly choking on it as he swallowed.

River sat on the couch and Storm joined her, though he tried to keep a sliver of space between them. He wanted to press close, to pull her to him until there was no space between them. But River seemed uncomfortable with him and he wouldn't force things.

They'd have time. Eventually.

He hoped.

"Did anything happen last night?" she asked and then hurried to add, "I mean, with the mercenaries."

"Not that I heard."

She slumped down, shoulders hunched over, and sucked in shuddering breaths. He thought he heard her muttering something, but she was too quiet for him to make out the shape of the words. After a moment, she straightened. "So I'm stuck here, there are bad guys with our friends, and our only hope of getting help is if you leave me here and fly back to the city alone. Is that it? Maybe you should go."

She was trembling so hard the vibrations traveled through the couch and touched him. It didn't take a genius to realize she didn't want to be left alone.

"Not yet." It should have been the first option, but now it felt like a last resort. He wasn't letting River fall into the hands of mercenaries if he could stop it. "I need to scout the area we covered last night, see what's going on. Maybe there's something we missed in the dark. You'll be safe. I won't be long."

Her hand darted out and grabbed his, squeezing it tight. And then after a silent moment, she let go and stood up. "Good luck."

RIVER LASTED all of ten minutes in the cabin after Storm left. It was his fault, really. If he hadn't given her that massage the night before, her muscles would be all tight and painful. She wouldn't have been able to move so easily.

Instead, she had energy thrumming through her and needed to find a way to expend it.

She promised herself she'd stay around the house. The night before, the surveillance drones had stopped long before they'd gotten to the cottage, so she doubted it was likely she'd be discovered. And she wasn't completely useless, she knew what the drones sounded like and would hide if she heard one.

If she stayed in the house, she'd go crazy with worry. Storm was walking back into danger to try and figure out what was going on. Worry buzzed in her veins, far greater than there should have been for a man she'd known for a handful of days and had exactly one conversation with before last night.

But apparently logic didn't care. There was something special about Storm, something that called to her.

And she wouldn't want anyone to get hurt.

She hadn't been able to see it last night, but there was a decent sized garden behind the cottage, and she spotted plants laden with huge vegetables that looked ripe for the plucking. River's fingers itched and she was tempted, but she stayed away. She wasn't familiar with the plant life on this planet and for all she knew, what looked like a cucumber could actually be a carnivorous plant.

Flowers lined some of the beds and she breathed deep. If she closed her eyes for a moment, she could pretend she was at some hidden getaway, just her and a hot dragon lord who was walking into danger to protect her.

Damn it. There went the fantasy.

She'd hoped there would be a garage or some place a vehicle might be hidden, but the cottage sat alone. She did find the small electric vehicle Storm had told her about the night before and gave it a close look. But there was no built-in communicator or anything else they could use to call for help. And River wasn't an expert in the languages of the Dominion, but she was pretty sure the speed gauge on the vehicle indicated a top speed of twenty kilometers an hour.

Faster than they could walk, certainly, but with the open sides and slow speed, the mercenaries at the compound could chase them down in an instant.

They needed a real vehicle. Or backup.

River had promised herself she'd stay close to the cottage, but she ended up following the road leading out of it for a bit. She could still see the cottage, she reasoned, so it wasn't like she was far. It would only take her a minute to sprint back.

Five minutes of walking later, and she couldn't see the cabin anymore, but she didn't want to turn around. She was tempted to point herself towards the city and walk all day and night until she found it. If she didn't know Storm would be frantic with worry, she might have really done it.

Moving away from the mercenaries felt safer. Maybe the electric cart wasn't such a bad idea. It would take a few hours to drive a distance that a normal vehicle could cross in less than two or that one of their ships could fly in a handful of minutes, but they'd be safe.

Maybe.

She had to go back. What if there were mercenaries at the edge of this road to prevent anyone from entering the compound? She could be walking straight into a trap.

And when the trees cleared on one side of the road and it turned to the right, she thought for a moment that was what it was. But the vehicle on the grass beside the road didn't belong to the mercenaries, not unless they'd lost a fight with *something*.

The front was all smashed in and the vehicle had started to rust. The windows were broken and one of the doors was dented and couldn't close all the way.

What could do that?

There were some animals in the outlands of Mayt that could chew up and spit out their land vehicles. Was this an animal? Or some other threat?

Whatever it was, it had been some time since the car had taken so much damage. She didn't know why it hadn't been cleared away, but it might just be the saving grace for her and Storm.

The dented door didn't open easily. Rust held it in its position and she had to wrench with all her strength to get inside. She winced at the screeching metal on metal sound as it opened and froze, certain that would call down a surveillance drone.

But nothing came.

The car smelled of nature and mold and the seats were kind of wet and gross. River pushed through the revulsion.

There was a mount for a communicator in the center of the console, but no communicator. Of course she wouldn't be that lucky. But River refused to be discouraged. This car felt like some kind of miracle and she was going to search ever centimeter of it for something useful. She *had* to find something.

And a minute later, she did. She followed a wire under the console to a small, circular device mounted under where the communicator would have sat. It wasn't lit up, but she didn't see any damage, either.

An emergency beacon.

River carefully pulled on wires until she extracted it and then slid out of the car. She didn't try to close the door, she didn't want the sound summoning anyone to her.

She headed straight back towards the cottage. Hopefully Storm would already be back.

But he wasn't. River's walk had taken a half hour or so, she refused to start worrying just yet. That resolve lasted three minutes. Worry set in, and she looked at the beacon to distract herself. They were some distance from the compound, and Storm could only move so fast, especially since he wouldn't risk transforming into a dragon and flying where anyone could see him.

She set the beacon on the kitchen counter and stared at it.

It didn't look like much, a small, dark sphere with a wire coming out the back. There should have been a switch or a button somewhere to manually activate it, but she didn't see one. It didn't matter. She wouldn't activate the beacon without first talking to Storm.

If he came back.

No. *When* he came back.

She didn't know who the beacon would alert. Some were short range and targeted the nearest settlements. Given where she was now, that could mean it would only message the compound. Not good. Most beacons were connected to emergency services or the beacon owner's family, sometimes both. At least that was how it worked back home. Maybe the Dominion was different.

The door slammed open and River spun around, her hands automatically going in front of her as if she were about to throw a punch. But it wasn't a mercenary.

Storm stumbled in, a bruise blooming on his face and his shirt torn. He took two steps and collapsed to the ground.

THE FIRST THING Storm felt as he rose to consciousness were warm hands on his naked chest. He stayed still, letting the feel of them soak into him. Mmmm, River. He wanted her to touch him everywhere, to see what the feel of her did to him. It wouldn't take much for his body to show her exactly how he was feeling.

He rolled to the side and her hands gripped at him to keep him in place as pain ripped through his body. Something cool pressed against his swollen eye.

Right. Pain.

Memory came surging back.

Storm cracked an eye open and saw River kneeling over him, face a mask of worry as she pulled things out of a first aid kit and used them on him.

"Don't waste it, I'm fine." His throat was scratchy

and the words sounded like they'd been tortured out of him. He felt like he'd fallen off a cliff and his body was only catching up to the pain it should be feeling.

The cliff wasn't far off.

River's worry turned into a glare and she held up two syringes. "I had to give you two doses of pain killer before you stopped whimpering. You're covered in bruises and you're lucky your leg isn't broken. What happened?"

Her hand was still on him. Storm liked that. He covered it with his own as he sat, keeping her close by him.

His life hadn't flashed before his eyes or any of that nonsense as he'd scrambled through the forest and tried to evade the mercenaries. But he'd had regrets. Number one among them that he'd never kissed his mate.

He could lean in now and steal that kiss. And if his chest and abs hurt just a little less, he might have tried. But he was worried she might push him back down and accuse him of feverish delirium.

The first time he kissed her, he wanted her to know he meant it.

Storm looked down at himself to assess the damage. Bruises mottled his skin and bandages covered several large swaths of it. He could feel the tell-tale burn of a cheap healing cream. All his muscles were stiff and his head still rang with a bit of a headache, despite the painkillers. They must not have put the good stuff in that first aid kit.

His shirt lay in chopped up tatters beside him. If he'd been with a dragon, he would have thought she had clawed it off him. Instead River must have used a knife or shears.

"What happened?" she asked again. "Let me get you some water." She tried to pull away, but he clutched her hand to him.

"Stay, it's okay." Water would probably feel wonderful right now, but not if it meant letting his mate go. "I scouted too close to the compound. They've armed the surveillance drones."

"What?" This time she tore her hand away, eyes wide with an accusation she didn't speak.

"I didn't think I was that close," he was quick to say. "I didn't lead them here."

"I didn't say you did." She pushed off the floor and marched into the kitchen, coming back after a moment with the promised water. Then she backed up and leaned against a wall, keeping distance between them.

No mate for him, then.

Storm struggled to his feet and sat back down on the couch. At least it was better than the floor. "I was right up on the border of the property before I realized it. There's a path to the east of the cottage that has a more direct route back. I got a better count of the mercs, a handful were on patrol outside, though they didn't look very alert. I must have tripped an alarm of some kind. Before I knew it, a drone was on me and it hit me with a blast. Not as strong as a blaster, but enough to bruise. I started running. It hit me again and I fell down a ravine, that's where I tore up my leg. I shot flame at it, but I missed. It's still out there."

"So they know we're out here."

"They know about me," he corrected. "The only way they'd know about you is if any of our people told them."

"Am I supposed to hope they killed our people so they didn't talk?" She crossed her arms in front of herself and held tight.

"I saw some of our people through a window. They were definitely alive." He turned in his seat and winced as he pulled on something. He should have been investigating in his warrior form, it could take more damage. But holding that form took concentration and he'd been too focused on his mission.

River rushed over and scooped up the first aid kit, sitting beside him on the couch and rifling through it. She held up the healing cream container. "Where does it hurt?"

It was nothing, the merest tweak of a bruise. But his mate was offering to put her hands on him, even though anger clearly simmered within her. Storm would be a fool to resist.

"On my side," he said, and turned closer to her to give her better access.

Healing creams were simple products designed to speed up healing times. Storm was used to the top of the market regen gel which could heal just about anything in a matter of hours. He wasn't sure the cream that River was using would do anything more than make his bruises burn unpleasantly for a while.

She smoothed her palm over the naked flesh of his side, gentle over the bruise that was forming there. Despite the pain in the rest of his body, Storm savored the touch. River moved with efficient swipes, covering the whole bruise in three passes. Then her hand stilled, but she didn't move away.

It was almost an embrace. If Storm leaned in closer and wrapped his arm around her, there would be no mistaking it. He had River right where he wanted her, and this time she wasn't going to back away.

She looked up at him, eyes big and framed by thick eyelashes. She was breathing hard and her tongue darted out to wet her lips, temptation incarnate.

Storm raised his hand to cup her cheek. He moved slowly, telegraphing the move and giving her plenty of time to pull away. If she did, he didn't know if he could stop himself from chasing her. But River stayed as she was, and when his palm met her cheek, she nuzzled against it, skin soft and warm.

He leaned in and she met him, their lips coming

together in a kiss so gentle it belied the want raging through him. If he wasn't injured, if they weren't in danger, if, if, if. He couldn't throw her down on the couch and have his way with her, not yet.

But he swept his tongue in her mouth and met hers in a tangle of need that couldn't be denied.

River moaned against him and her hand curled against his side, making his bruise burn even more. He didn't care. It was proof his mate was here with him, that the need was as much hers as it was his own. No amount of pain could make him back away from this.

And whatever sense he had that told him he couldn't take her right there was quickly diminishing. Their enemies didn't know where they were. And he was well enough to pleasure his mate.

But after a moment of desperate kissing, River managed to pull back. Her lips were wet and red and tempting enough he almost leaned forward and tugged her back to him. Almost.

"There's something I have to show you," she said.

COULD A KISS MAKE YOU DRUNK? River had trouble walking in a straight line for the three steps it took her to get to the kitchen counter. Her entire body buzzed with pleasure and she didn't know how she'd managed to pull away.

It was either the smartest or stupidest move of her entire life.

She had a dragon lord on the couch kissing her like she was his whole world. His body was on fire under her fingers, but she was pretty sure it wasn't a fever. His hands had been that hot the night before.

Surrendering to his touch, to his kiss, was a guarantee of pleasure. And what a story she'd have, of the time she'd run from mercenaries and made love to an aristocratic dragon.

But already she could feel her stupid heart wanting

more. She had no right to ask or wish. They were quite literally from two different worlds. A dragon had no reason to want a simple former teacher who was playing, and failing, at being a diplomat. She couldn't exactly call it a success when the rest of her crew were currently hostages.

And there was another reason nothing could happen. How could they do that when their colleagues were in danger from a group of vicious mercenaries?

If anyone found out about it, she'd be a laughingstock. Or a pariah. The woman who cared more about a fuck than saving her people.

"Is everything alright?" Storm asked.

Her mind had wandered. River scooped up the beacon and squared her shoulders. She was going to do this, the job, and not get all wrapped up in Storm.

That resolve lasted until she turned around and remembered he was shirtless. He sat on the couch like some sort of sensual king waiting for his subject to approach. And as tempting as it was to kneel before his throne, River forced herself to thrust the beacon out in front of her to see.

"I went exploring myself," she admitted. "Away from the compound. I found a wrecked vehicle. No communicator, but there was this."

Smoke swirled around Storm. "You went out? Do you see what they did to *me*? What do you think they would do to you?" He took deep breaths and the smoke began to dissipate.

"I'm not the one who got chased by drones. And I needed to do something. I'm not the wait at home quietly type." Her job wasn't dangerous back home, but she wasn't afraid of hard work. And she'd had to do something to keep herself from going crazy.

Storm's eyes raked over her, but this time it wasn't sexual. He was reassuring himself she was safe.

"I didn't see anyone," she said. "I walked perhaps a kilometer, maybe a kilometer and a half. The vehicle is on the road that leads to the city, and it's been there for some time. Maybe it was in a collision with another vehicle, maybe it hit an animal. It certainly wasn't the product of these mercenaries. Not unless they've been lurking in these woods for months or more."

"Recon could take that long," he grumbled. "But that doesn't sound like any kind of trap I've heard of. Can I see it?"

She handed over the beacon and he examined it, first rolling it around in his hands before holding it up close as if he'd developed x-ray vision and could divine its secrets. Hell, maybe he did have x-ray vision. He was a dragon, he could easily be hiding super powers.

"I don't see any damage," he said. "What was it plugged into?"

"Center console. I unplugged it. It wasn't lit up or

anything. That vehicle lost power a long time ago. I don't know if it was ever activated." Beacons could be used more than once, but they weren't like communicators. If the person who'd been in the accident survived, they would have thought to grab their communicator, but there was no reason to grab the beacon.

"This should plug into one of the outlets in this cabin. Then we'll be able to find the manual override." But he didn't make to get up off of the couch and plug the device in.

"Any idea who we'll be calling?" Maybe he knew more about the Dominion than she did. She wouldn't be so hesitant if she wasn't afraid of alerting the mercenaries to their presence.

"There's only one way to find out." He handed the beacon over to her. "Do you want to do the honors?"

She took it from him and found the nearest plug. The beacon plugged in easily, and after a moment a light started blinking. "It's powering up." After a moment, the light stopped blinking and remained solid. "I think it's on."

"Do you see a switch?"

"No." She looked at it from every angle, careful not to unplug it, but there was nothing.

"See if it opens," he suggested.

She'd tried to pry it open earlier, and it hadn't budged. Not wanting to break it, she'd given up. She tried again and still nothing, until lights on the side of the beacon seemed to indicate she should twist.

That popped it right open, and inside there was a small red button.

River looked over at Storm and flashed it towards him. "Last chance to stop me."

"Do it."

For some reason, following the order was easier than doing it by herself. She wasn't someone who needed a boss, needed to be told what to do. But when the stakes were this high, she didn't want to be the only one making decisions.

She pressed the button.

The light started blinking again.

River stared at it, waiting for some other indication it was working, but the light just kept blinking. "Well, that's anticlimactic." She set it down gently on the floor and moved away. "I guess it will be a while until we know if we're saved."

Rather than join Storm back on the couch, she found a chest of drawers and opened them. Inside were a pile of gray shirts that must have belonged to the groundskeeper. She unfolded one and held it up. The fit might be tight, but at least Storm would be covered.

Even with the bruises and bandages, his chest was a temptation she couldn't keep resisting.

She held the shirt out to Storm, but instead of

taking it from her, he tugged on it until she was hovering right over him. She could have let go of the shirt, but something wild inside of her wouldn't let her, especially not when he was looking at her like that.

All the thoughts for why they shouldn't do anything evaporated and she couldn't recall a single one.

She didn't really care.

The shirt fell to the ground as Storm ran his hands through her hair and pulled her down to him. River was powerless to resist. She climbed onto the couch, carefully straddling him and not giving him too much of her weight, conscious of his injuries.

Their mouths crashed together and the heat consumed her.

CHAPTER
THIRTEEN

HE DIDN'T KNOW how long they'd been kissing on that tiny couch, but Storm was content to let the rest of the world fall away so long as he had River in his arms. It might have been alarming how she'd gone from a stranger to the person he craved above all others in a blink of time, but he didn't care.

She was his.

And he had to protect her.

He wasn't sure what alerted him, but he tore himself away, clutching her hips tight to keep her from moving.

"Quiet." He barely breathed the word, but River clamped her kiss-swollen lips shut.

The shutters were down, so no one could see inside the cabin, but that meant they couldn't see out. Storm strained to hear, but there was nothing. Maybe he was just overreacting.

No.

There was *nothing*.

All day he'd heard the sounds of insects and animals throughout the woods around them, evidence that life went on even while his own people were in turmoil. Now those insects, birds, and other critters were as quiet as death.

Something was out there. And it was dangerous.

The beacon was still blinking on the floor, and he didn't think it had been long enough for help to come from the city. He might have been followed from the compound. Or the mercenaries could have picked up the beacon's signal. Whoever was outside, he didn't think they were friendly.

River eased off of him and Storm stood. He pulled the shirt she'd found for him over his head to cover his naked chest. He didn't want to fight these people at a disadvantage.

There was only the front door, and if he were running this op, they'd have blasters trained on it and ready to fire the moment he appeared. Then they'd charge in and secure the place. So the front door was out.

There was a small window on the other side of the house. It was a risk of its own. If there were enough people out there, they could be covering the entire house. He'd be in an even more precarious position diving through the window than walking out the door.

But it had to be done.

"Take cover," he told River. "If they take me or…" He couldn't say it out loud, not when he'd finally found his mate. "If they take me, dive out the back window and run into the woods. Head for the city. It'll be a long walk, but you should be able to do it."

She reached out and squeezed his hand. She didn't say a word.

He didn't know if that was agreement with his plan, but there was no more time. The longer they had to investigate, the more chance there was that they'd breach the building. And he wasn't letting that happen.

He carefully eased open the shutter, wincing at every slight scrape of metal on metal. Then he opened the window. It was a tight fit, but he slithered through. And once he was outside, he summoned his warrior form. He wasn't in his dragon shape. Instead, his human skin had developed thin scales that would defend him from blaster shots, his hands ended in claws, and it was easier to summon his flame.

Dragon lore had it that one man in warrior form could hold off an army. Storm hoped the legends were true.

He crept around the side of the building until he spotted the mercenaries. Two of them, armed to the teeth, and studying the front of the cabin. One had his blaster trained on the door.

Only two?

No need to fight that army today.

The healing cream had done its job and he was no longer aching from the wounds he'd suffered earlier. But he wasn't going to let these two mercs do any more damage to him. And certainly not to River.

Storm summoned his flame and cast it at the mercenary holding the blaster with a roar. His fire caught onto something explosive and the first mercenary screamed and dropped in a pile of smoke and ash.

The second mercenary put up more of a fight. He had some kind of force field that deflected some of Storm's flame, and he managed to get a couple of shots off with his own blaster. But Storm wasn't playing. He didn't let up on the fire and after a moment, the force field was overwhelmed and flickered out. Storm's flame kissed the mercenary and he screamed.

Instead of letting it consume the man, Storm pulled it back. He wanted to annihilate this piece of scum, but he had to know what was going on, and this mercenary provided the perfect opportunity.

While the man writhed on the ground, Storm grabbed his weapons and kicked them out of range. The man had brought his own flexible restraints. Storm had to shift out of his warrior form to handle the material, but he secured the man's hands behind his back and his feet together with ease. He wasn't getting away.

River opened the door when he asked, and the relief on her face was palpable. Then she realized he had a prisoner. "What are you doing?"

"We need some questions answered." He dragged the man into the small bathroom and dumped him in the tub. It would be easier to secure him in there, though not tenable in anything approaching the long term.

He took another flexible tie and secured the man's hands to a metal bar on the wall of the shower. It was a little too high for him to sit comfortably, so he'd have to semi-crouch if he didn't want to torture his own shoulders.

Good.

The man was only half-conscious, and no doubt planned to stay that way. Storm wouldn't put up with that. He turned on the water in the shower and watched as his prisoner sputtered awake.

Storm turned the water off.

River stood in the door to the bathroom. He wanted to tell her to leave, that she didn't need to see this, but right now all he planned to do was ask questions. She deserved to hear the answers.

"How did you two off worlders get a Dominion emergency beacon?" the mercenary demanded once the water had finished dripping down his face.

That answered that. They'd known the beacon might have given them away. At least they'd only sent two mercs to check it out.

"Answer my questions and you don't need to die." Storm said it calmly, the same voice he'd learned from his trainers at the Academy. A dragon in charge of his surroundings and his enemy didn't need to rely on threats.

"Hey, man, this is a job. I'll die in battle, but I'm not here for this bullshit. Tell me what you want to know and we're good." He tried to readjust himself, but his bound and secured hands kept him firmly in place.

"How many people are holding the facility?" Storm had a count of his own, but he knew it wasn't complete.

The man thought for a moment. "There's twenty of us. Well, nineteen now."

Eighteen in total, when Storm was done with this guy. Not good odds. "What was your objective?"

"Get in, secure the hostages, kill the human leader. Get out before the authorities get back." He recited the mission quickly, as if betraying his fellows was nothing to him.

Or was he lying? Storm couldn't verify a word he said, and he couldn't take it as the truth.

"Why?"

That wasn't his question. River's word broke over them, and Storm forced himself not to glance at her.

The why didn't matter, not right now. But she wasn't a soldier, and it was her people being targeted.

"I don't get paid to ask that question," said the merc. "Contract came in for him, we do the job."

"Is Seth dead?" River's voice trembled as she asked.

The mercenary didn't answer immediately so Storm summoned a lick of flame to his palm, a promise of the pain he could inflict. The mercenary swallowed thickly. "He was alive when we left to investigate the beacon."

"Why?" That was Storm's question, even though he was trying not to care about whys. "You've had plenty of time to kill him."

"The contract wanted a dragon to do it."

Oh, that was bad. Really bad. And it meant that no one was supposed to come out of this mess alive. Storm could see how it would play out. Either they'd convince one of his people to kill the human, possibly on the promise that the dragons could go free, or they'd stage the death of Seth to look draconic. Then they'd murder everyone else so there wouldn't be any witnesses.

And they'd start a war between the humans of Mayt and the dragons of Vemion.

"Who hired you?" He didn't expect the man to know, but he had to try and find out. The stakes had just risen beyond anything he could imagine, and if they didn't stop this plot, no one was safe.

"How should I know?"

"Do you normally work in the Dominion?" Crime was punished harshly, and most mercs skated to the edge of legality, some dancing over it with all the grace of a rampaging beast. But even the Dominion needed mercs.

"Not recently."

He had more questions, trying to figure out where this crew's loyalties lay. By the time he was done, Storm was almost certain the orders didn't come from anyone official in the Dominion. Someone was trying to start a war. The Dominion would always be a suspect. If the dragons and humans went to war, they'd go a long way to destroying one another. Then the Dominion could swoop in and claim their two planets for its growing empire.

But complex assassination plots weren't the Dominion's style. If Storm had to wager, he'd say this hit had come from either Mayt or Vemion. He could figure out why later.

He was out of questions to ask and the sun was getting low. When this man and his companion didn't report back to their people, more would be sent. Storm and River were no longer safe in the little cottage and they'd have to act.

Storm looked at his prisoner and then back over his shoulder at River. "You should leave the room."

THE MAN in the tub struggled at Storm's declaration. River didn't know his name. In all the questions Storm had asked, that one had never come up.

She knew why he wanted her to leave the room. He might have said the mercenary would live if he answered questions, but he'd been lying.

"I'm not leaving," she said. She didn't want to see a man die. She didn't want Storm to be forced into doing this. He'd already dealt death to the man he'd killed outside. But that had been a fight. This would be murder. Their prisoner was tied up securely. He couldn't defend himself.

And they couldn't let him get away.

She knew it all without needing to be told. If they let the man go, he'd run right back to his masters and report back about her and Storm. If they left the cottage and left him tied up, he might eventually get free. Or he'd starve where he was tied in the shower, and a quick death would be its own kindness.

But it still felt wrong.

She wouldn't let Storm carry this burden alone.

"You promised!" the prisoner writhed against his restraints. "I answered your questions. What are you doing?"

River flinched at the words, but Storm's face was completely devoid of emotions. "I'll do it outside. No need to contaminate the cabin."

She couldn't tell him he wasn't a killer. That was patently false. And she couldn't say he didn't need to do this. They were vulnerable enough as it was. But her stomach roiled in disgust at herself. She was a good person. She didn't murder people.

And yet, here she was. Letting it happen.

Storm cut the restraint tying the man's hands to the bar and hauled him out of the tub. His feet were bound together and he could barely shuffle. He resisted at first, until Storm threatened to carry him.

"Loosen my feet and I'll walk," he said. "But I can hardly move."

Storm hesitated for a moment, but he undid the ties at the man's feet and let him walk.

In the front of the cottage, the evidence of Storm's fight with the mercenaries lay all around them. There were blasters on the ground, and the steaming pile of ash that used to be the other mercenary. River didn't look too close, afraid she might see something to remind her that had once been a person.

Storm had to do it. He was protecting them both. But it was still difficult to see.

"You're going to do it just like that?" the mercenary demanded. "Not even going to offer a fight? At least let me die like a man." He was spitting defiance at them, wounded pride, and all of it masking fear.

River couldn't blame him. In the same situation she'd be sobbing in terror.

Storm blocked off the path that led back to the compound. The man had nowhere to run, and no weapons to fight with. He was several meters from the nearest fallen blaster.

It was over.

Storm summoned his flame and held it in his palm. River had to force herself not to look away from this. He was protecting them both. It had to be witnessed.

Storm was hesitating and River didn't blame him. She may not have known him well, but they both knew this was wrong, even if there was no other choice. Part of her wished she could do it for him, but she knew if it was up to her, she would try and find a way to keep the man alive.

Even though it would doom them both.

She didn't realize what was happening until Storm yelled. The man lunged to the side, diving towards one of the blasters even though it should have been too far away. To get to the woods and run, he'd have to go around Storm.

Instead, he sprang to his feet and lunged for her.

She didn't have time to think or scream. All she could do was react. She held her hands up in front of her and thought about the fire in Storm's hands. It shouldn't have done anything. She wasn't a dragon.

And yet.

Fire streamed out of her human hands and caught him in the chest. He stumbled backwards, clutching at the smoking hole. His eyes met hers, wide and disbelieving, before he crumpled to the ground and lay still.

River couldn't do anything but stare at the fallen man. The man that *she* had somehow killed with fire from *her* hands. It wasn't possible. It shouldn't have been. She was a normal person. No special powers, no nothing.

She looked over at Storm who was just as still as her. "What the hell just happened?" she demanded.

And then she puked.

IF STORM NEEDED any more evidence that River was his mate, there it was. She'd channeled his flame as if it were her own.

He rushed forward and held her hair back as she emptied the contents of her stomach. He didn't ask if it was her first kill, he knew it must have been. When she was done, he ushered her inside and poured her a glass of water.

She washed out her mouth and then slowly sipped the rest. "I killed him." It came out a whisper.

"He was going to kill you." He wanted to hold her tight and assure her that everything would be okay. But there were two dead mercenaries in front of the cabin with eighteen more back at the compound. They didn't have a lot of time for reassurances.

"How did you do that?" She pushed her glass away

and looked up at him, eyes wide and gleaming with unshed tears. "How did you make it so I could shoot flame? Is there something wrong with you?"

"Not a bit." He wrapped her in his arms and held her close. She fit like she'd been made for him, the piece of his soul he'd been missing forever. "I did it the same way I let you hold the light the other night." That wasn't a lie, not exactly. But it wasn't the truth either.

He couldn't give her the truth right now. Not if he was going to protect her.

"We need to leave," he said gently. They couldn't stall any longer, even though he knew River's hands would still tremble when he let go of her. "They know where we are now, and they're going to be sending someone to look for those guys. We can't be here when they get here."

River looked up at him, her eyes wide with fear but also with a fierce determination. She wasn't a warrior, but she had a core of steel inside of her, and she wasn't about to give up now. "I think we should wait right here and greet them when they show up."

An immediate denial was on his tongue, but Storm forced himself to consider it. They'd handled two mercs easily enough, except for a bit of emotional upheaval. "We don't know how many they'll send. We can't be in the cabin." It might have felt safe, four walls and a roof all around them, but they were trapped in it.

"I may not be a soldier, but I can think for myself.

They don't have a lot of people to spare, especially if they're holding six people, including three dragons, hostage," she pointed out. She pulled out of his arms but laced her fingers with his as she spoke. "How many can they afford to send? Four? Maybe? They'll know something happened to their people when they don't get on comms, but they won't know what. They *don't* know we're out here, they just know someone raised a beacon."

"You want to set a trap." Storm let the idea roll around in his mind for a bit. "It could work. But we need to see what supplies that shed out back has. And we need to work fast."

"Then let's go."

He did his best to block the view of the fallen mercenaries as they left the cabin and sent River to the shed while he took what weapons he could from the dead. Two blasters, four knives. Not a huge bounty, but better than they'd been.

He hoped River knew how to fire a blaster.

When he met her at the shed, she had the rope they would need and more in a pile. Storm took a look of his own and grabbed a few more things. They didn't have time to get elaborate, but the trap didn't need to be.

He handed the blaster over to River and she took it and examined it with the kind of efficiency that indicated she knew what she was doing. She slipped it into her pocket. "Target practice is pretty popular," she explained. "I'm no expert, but I can shoot."

Could she shoot a person? He didn't ask. Instead, he handed over the second blaster as well. "I have my flame. You keep these."

She took it, but didn't put it in her pocket for a moment. "Am I going to spontaneously shoot fire again?"

Once they had a moment of peace, he'd teach her how to harness his flame. Of course, he'd probably wait until after they'd slaked themselves in his bed. "It's instinctual right now. If you reach for my flame, you'll probably summon it. But without control. And it won't always work. The blasters will. Use them."

"There's something you're not telling me about the flame." It wasn't a question.

He had to tread carefully here. He didn't want to lie, didn't want to do anything that might interrupt their future happiness. But his instincts were screaming at him that the truth would scare her too much. "There is," he admitted, choosing his words carefully. "It's nothing bad, but I fear it's… a distraction. You have my word that I'll tell you all once we're safe. Please trust me in this."

"For some reason I do." She let it drop.

They hauled their material to the path the two

mercenaries had taken. It was hard work to set everything up so that the traps were barely visible to the naked eye, and when they were done, they were both covered in sweat.

Would it be enough?

"We have to take them out the moment they trip the traps," he warned her. "We can't give them a chance to call for help or fire at us. Stay back and let me do it."

She pulled out one of her blasters and backed up with a nod.

The traps were set up and there was nothing but the waiting. Behind him, River was so quiet he might have forgotten she was there if her presence didn't burn brightly in his consciousness.

No. He'd always know exactly where she was when she was near him.

After a while, doubt began to creep in. Had the mercenaries noticed their men were gone? Did they care? What if instead of sending out another small team they decided to bomb the place to deal with any potential problem?

These kinds of worries were why Storm had never made a particularly good soldier. He'd done his best at the Academy and he'd served when he'd been commanded. But everyone had been more than happy when his contract finished and he chose not to renew.

Then he heard a noise. Behind him, River jolted, but she froze back into place just as quickly.

Here they were.

The mercenaries came into view a minute later and Storm let his flame grow under his skin. It would take no effort to incinerate anyone in his path. His only concern was that he didn't also take the forest out with him.

Come on, come on, he wanted to say out loud, but he didn't dare breathe while he waited for them to cross the first trap. They were close. Three more steps and he was sure they'd have them.

And then the two mercenaries stopped.

He could feel River vibrating with tension behind him, but he didn't spare her a look, no matter how much he wanted to reassure her—and perhaps himself—that all would be well.

Though waiting in the trees to kill unsuspecting mercenaries was far from well.

At the very least, it would all be over soon.

The two mercenaries exchanged a flurry of hand signs that Storm didn't understand. Had they seen the traps? He thought he'd hidden them well, but with limited time and resources, he couldn't be sure.

The hand motions grew even more rapid, until one of the mercenaries threw their hands up in obvious frustration, spun on a heel, and marched straight into the first trap.

The second mercenary whipped out his weapon, aiming anywhere he could see, but it was too late.

Storm unleashed his fire and it was done.

Behind him, River made a sound in the back of her throat. Storm finally let himself turn to look at her. She'd gone a bit pale and he feared she might vomit again, but she met his eyes steadily and nodded.

"That's four mercenaries down," she said. "I'm not sure our luck will hold out if they send another team. I think we should bring this fight to them."

Two against sixteen, and only one of those two a trained fighter. The odds were terrible, but they'd improve with the element of surprise and if they could free the hostages.

He didn't want her to come with him. The mission would be dangerous. The mercenaries had planned their swift takeover of the compound and pulled it off with terrifying efficiency. Unless every single thing went right, taking the compound back would end in bloodshed. Maybe death.

But the cabin wasn't safe anymore. No place was. And they didn't know if their distress beacon had reached anyone but the mercenaries.

"Can you shoot someone if you have to? Not just in a panic. Not just instinct. Really do it." He'd seen trained soldiers freeze on battlefield simulations, unable to do the deed even when they knew that their enemy was a bit of computer code.

"We're going to survive this," she said with

surprising intensity. "And then you and me are going to have a talk. And more."

Fire that had nothing to do with his flame roared through him. There was no time for intimacy when anyone might be coming for them. But when this was over, River wasn't getting away from him.

Ever.

CHAPTER
SIXTEEN

COULD RIVER REALLY SHOOT someone if it came to that? The blaster was heavy in her hands as they hiked back towards the compound on the shorter path that Storm had found earlier in the day.

Had that really just been a few hours ago?

It didn't seem possible. This whole week was something out of a twisted nightmare. The kind of nightmare she'd want to go back to again and again just so she could spend a minute with her dragon lord.

He wasn't really hers. And he'd admitted to hiding things from her. But she wanted him more than she'd ever wanted anyone, and even her heart was fluttering at the idea of him.

It should have been the furthest thing from her mind. They were about to mount an assault on a heavily armed compound with nothing but weapons they'd scavenged from mercenaries and Storm's innate firepower.

If they survived this, she might start believing in miracles.

And if they survived, she was going to be brave enough to take Storm to bed. She could take on mercenaries. She could kill. Surely that meant she could find the courage to invite a dragon lord who she already knew liked her into her bed.

A man didn't kiss like that when he didn't want someone.

The trees began to thin out and Storm rushed her into the underbrush where they ducked down and hid as a surveillance drone flew overhead. She was tempted to shoot it down, but they were relying on the element of surprise. They'd have to be mindful of the drones for now.

Another one flew over a minute after the first, but they didn't see any more by the time they made it to the edge of the compound property.

Now the fear got to River. She clutched her blaster like it was some sort of stuffed animal, but it didn't give comfort, only the promise of violence.

That would have to be enough.

She and Storm huddled close together as they looked over the property. "Four by the shuttles," he said quietly as he pointed them out. "I don't see any more outside. Do you?"

She looked, but she didn't have a practiced eye at spotting soldiers. She shook her head. "None."

"If we can, we want to leave at least one shuttle intact for an escape. We'll destroy them all if we must and call in reinforcements, but I'd rather not rely on Dominion kindness."

"Agreed." The Dominion had failed them once, they didn't need to try their luck again.

"I'm going around to flank them. You stay here. At my signal, start blasting. Don't worry about hitting anyone, and don't shoot me. I can handle those four, but I want them distracted. If anyone comes out of the buildings, shoot at them for as long as you can, but move before they find you. And they will find you quick. Retreat into the woods if you have to. Got it?" He was looking at her with utter confidence.

That made one of them. But River forced herself to nod.

Storm's serious face transformed into a grin, and he leaned in close and stole a quick kiss. "You've got this. You have to. We have a date."

Then, before she could react to that, he was gone.

Only when he'd disappeared from sight did she realize he'd never said what his signal was meant to be.

"You'll figure it out," she muttered to herself. He was a dragon, he probably meant fire.

She knew the general range of a blaster, and unfortunately, it meant she couldn't stay where she was if she hoped to land any shots against anyone. The mercenary's weapons could have been a higher grade than she was used to using, but she doubted they somehow got double the range. And the closer a person was to their target, the more accurate and painful the blast was. The force dissipated over long distances, which was why few snipers liked blasters. There were other weapons for that.

She hadn't mentioned to Storm that the only reason she knew as much about blasters as she did was that an ex-boyfriend of hers had been obsessed with them. She'd spent a summer learning all she could about them in the hopes of impressing him. The guy was long gone, but the knowledge remained.

And hopefully that knowledge would give her a chance at a future, or at least a night, with her dragon lord.

River looked out for any incoming surveillance drones, but she didn't see or hear any. Her best chance at cover was a cluster of land vehicles parked near the main building of the compound. But running there would put her in the open.

How long would it take for Storm to get into position?

She forced herself to move. Stalling would only hurt them both. She stayed low and kept her eyes peeled, but no one spotted her.

A moment later, fire bloomed at the back of the mercenary ship.

River started firing wildly. That had to be the signal.

She'd only gotten off a few rounds when the makeshift front doors the mercenaries must have erected after blasting their way into the main compound building opened and two more mercenaries ran out. River turned her blaster on them without a thought and they both went down. Blaster fire was rarely lethal, but it could knock a human out for hours.

She was poised and ready for more to follow, but no one did. Not until she heard footsteps right next to her and swung around and aimed her blaster right at Storm's chest.

His hands went up in surrender, and she lowered the weapon.

"Six down," he said.

Ten more if their intel was right.

They took as many weapons as they could off the fallen mercenaries at the door. Those mercenaries were still breathing and a part of River was relieved, even as it complicated matters. One of the fallen mercenaries had flexible ties on his belt and Storm quickly used them to bind the two mercenaries together, back to back. Then he bound their hands and feet to a decorative fixture made of thick metal that was just outside the door.

It was eerily quiet inside. Technically no more quiet than it had been on the days while they'd been negotiating, but there was another quality to the air that changed the tenor of the silence.

Desperation.

Fear.

They didn't meet any more mercenaries in the first hall or the second. There had to be surveillance cameras, and she and Storm weren't trying to hide.

Then they heard footsteps. They were coming up on another corridor and there was no place to hide. Storm had a blaster of his own now and he raised it. River forced her hands into the proper position.

As soon as they had eyes on the dark uniforms of the mercenaries, Storm fired. River couldn't make herself pull the trigger.

It didn't matter. The mercenaries fell.

They had a few leftover ties, but there was nothing to tie them to. She and Storm divested the unconscious mercenaries of their weapons and bound them together. It wouldn't hold them forever, but at least they'd be inconvenienced.

Eight more mercenaries. Maybe.

They passed through the hallways that led to the sleeping quarters, getting closer to the heart of the compound.

Two more mercenaries walked the halls. Two more went down.

"They can't be monitoring security feeds." River couldn't hold the observation back anymore. Both sets of guards had been unprepared for them. How?

"They may have cut the feed to make sure no one could get in remotely. And to make sure there is no evidence for when they leave," Storm explained.

It was a grim reminder of the stakes. If she and Storm failed, there could be a war on the horizon for their people. They had to stop it now.

Six guards left.

At the entrance to the negotiation room, they found four mercenaries lounging outside the door, holding their blasters negligently and slouching around. Were all mercenaries like this? Or had whoever hired them found the cheapest crew around?

This time the mercenaries managed to get a few shots off, and River heard Storm grunt as one made impact.

She'd hesitated to shoot before, but with the sound of Storm's pain in her ears she unleashed the power of the blaster on them. Two shots, two dropped mercenaries.

The third went down after two shots, but the fourth didn't fall until Storm hit him with a blast of fire.

They didn't bother to secure these mercenaries, not with the likelihood that their own people were right through the door. They busted inside, ready to fight whatever mercenaries were left, but froze when they saw the scene before them.

Two of the dragons, Night and Echo, had one of the mercenaries on the ground. Seth, Ash, and Will had tackled the other. Luke was a bit off to the side, not tangling in the fight. The other two dragons were standing back as well.

"We heard your rescue and decided to help out," the oldest of the dragons, Lore, informed them as one of the mercenaries shrieked. "Are they taken care of?" He sounded very calm for a person who'd just been held hostage for two days.

Storm nodded.

"Very well." Rush turned towards the dragons holding their mercenary. "Interrogate him."

For some reason, that sent the mercenary under the dragons into a fit of laughter. Night said something that River couldn't make out over the guffaws. And that mercenary's laugh sent a shiver down her spine.

"Why is he laughing?" she demanded. She strode forward. Rush might have wanted his people to do the questioning, but he didn't get to command her.

Something was wrong.

She pulled out her blaster and aimed it right at the mercenary. That made him laugh even harder. And finally, he calmed just enough to gasp out one word.

"Boom."

River's gaze snapped back to Storm, but he was

already moving. One of the tables was still covered in a table cloth, and he pulled it back to reveal a hunk of tubes and wiring. River was no expert, but it looked like a bomb to her untrained eyes.

She was frozen for a moment until someone started yelling.

And then it was time to run.

CHAPTER
SEVENTEEN

STORM WAS BREATHING hard by the time the last of the hostages cleared the building, River among them. If he could have, he would have scooped her up and sprinted to make sure she was the first out, but he could see that she felt just as responsible for the safety of their people as he did.

Besides, she was probably faster by herself than he'd be if he had to carry her.

He expected the blast to hit as soon as they made it outside. He'd incapacitated the two remaining mercenaries with a shot of his blaster just so they couldn't cause trouble on the way out.

But there was no blast.

Was the bomb on a timer? If not, all the mercenaries were out of commission. It could have been nothing more than an empty threat, but Storm didn't think so.

A bomb would cover up the mercenaries' involvement quite nicely. Though he didn't know how they would manage to pin it all on the dragons if everyone was destroyed by a bomb. Perhaps they hoped the blast would look like dragon fire.

"To the ships!" Seth, the human leader, urged.

He had a point. If that bomb was real, they had to get as far away as they could.

None of the humans or dragons who'd been held prisoner seemed injured. There were a few superficial cuts and many of them were moving stiffly, but nothing worse than that. It made the escape easier, and they crossed to their ships with ease. Storm kept his eyes open for stray mercenaries, but he didn't see any.

By his count, they'd taken out all of them.

The humans boarded their ship. River was the last one outside, and she hesitated at the bottom of the ramp. She looked over at him and their eyes met. Storm wanted to demand that she come with him, that she abandon her human life to come be his bride on Vemion.

But there was no time for explanations.

He would come for her once they were safe.

River finally turned and boarded her ship, taking a piece of his heart with her.

Storm followed his people onto their shuttle. All of the dragons followed Rush into the cockpit. There was safety in numbers, and he understood the instinct.

Rush let out a stream of curses and slapped his hand against the dash.

"They've done something to disable the damned thing," he spat and followed it up with even more cursing.

Storm was impressed. He didn't think Rush knew those words. Instead, he was hearing a few he was unfamiliar with and filed them away for future use. So what if the acts Rush was describing were anatomically impossible? They sounded impressive.

"Move," Rush commanded once he'd finished his epithets. "Chase the humans before they leave."

They scurried off the ship, but the humans weren't on their craft. They stood on the tarmac and didn't seem surprised when the dragons joined them.

"They've disabled our launch system," said Ash. "We can probably fix it, but it will take time." He glanced back at the compound, which still hadn't exploded.

They were too close. Storm was certain of it. If he were going to blow a place up, he'd make sure he did it right. There'd be nothing but a smoking crater when he was done. The mercenaries hadn't been competent at anything else, but maybe they were surprisingly good at covering their tracks.

And they'd want to get off the planet alive.

"Onto the mercenary craft," Storm urged. He'd done some minor damage to it while taking out the guards, but ships were built to break atmo. They could take fire damage. "Now!"

That got everyone running again.

Storm muscled in front of everyone and raced to the cockpit, the certainty of their doom hanging over him. He closed the entrance ramp and engaged the defensive shields. They couldn't launch with the shields engaged, but that wasn't the important part, not at the moment.

He pulled up the external cameras and focused them on the building. Nothing looked out of the ordinary.

The two delegations packed into the cockpit with him. There was not enough room for ten people, but no one was willing to leave.

"What is the meaning of this?" Seth demanded. "Why aren't we launching?"

A blast rocked the ship, the shock wave strong enough to make them slide several meters along the concrete below.

Smoke engulfed what was left of the building. When it cleared, Storm doubted even a single wall would still be standing.

"Can we launch this ship?" River's voice cut through the grumblings all around them. "Because I think it's time to leave."

And that sent the delegations into an uproar.

CHAPTER
EIGHTEEN

THIS WAS FREAKING RIDICULOUS.

River listened to the two delegations argue for more than a minute, a headache growing in the back of her head. If she thought about the fact that a building had just exploded, she might go mad with fear. She could feel a whole host of emotions threatening to take her over, everything she'd been ignoring over the past few days.

But she couldn't do it here. They still weren't safe. Had they forgotten that?

"Hey!" she yelled loud enough to cut through the din. She still had her blaster in hand, but she wasn't about to shoot. The room was too crowded, and she wasn't going to damage their only way off planet.

Her shout turned all eyes her way.

She made eye contact with the dragon leader, Lore,

and spoke. "What's the problem?" Seth wouldn't like it, but if she only spoke to the humans, the dragons would object. Someone had to remember some freaking diplomacy.

Lore took her in, eyes flicking up and down. It wasn't a sexual perusal, not at all. But she had the strangest idea that he could see something about her that she couldn't. "We're trying to decide on a pilot. And a destination."

She had to bite back a groan. They could stay here arguing all week if someone didn't make them see sense.

To buy time, she took a headcount and realized something. "Where are the Domini facilitators? What happened to them?"

Seth answered. "They took off as soon as the mercs showed up. We hoped they were going for backup, but I suspect they were paid off."

An alarm started beeping on the dash, and one of the dragons leaned forward to read it before Ash got in his space and echoed what he was saying. The message was simple.

A ship was incoming.

"We need one dragon pilot and one human pilot in the cockpit," she declared, putting as much command into her voice as she could muster. She'd stood up to important city officials with this tone of voice, she could do it now. "Everyone else, go explore the ship.

Pilots, get us into space. Once we're clear of the Dominion, we can figure out where we're going. Can the life support systems keep us going for a couple days, Ash?"

He checked something on the dash and give her a firm nod.

"Right. There should be rations in the canteen. If not, we won't die in a day. Everyone out!" She waved her hands to herd the non-pilots out of the cockpit. There was a bit of grumbling, but surprisingly, Seth backed her up, commanding Luke and Will to go check out the supplies situation. That led Rush to command Echo to go check if there were any suitable sleeping quarters, and he went with her.

Ash and Night stayed in the cockpit, and she and Storm were left alone outside.

A minute later, Ash's voice came over the intercom system and instructed them to secure themselves for takeoff. She and Storm silently found seats. Once they were strapped in, he reached out a hand and she clutched him tight. The danger was past, except for the incoming ship. But as long as they could avoid that, they might actually be something approaching safe.

River wasn't sure she could believe it.

The ship jostled as it lifted off, and for a moment or two, gravity pressed down hard, making River feel like she was being flattened out. Then the feeling was gone as they broke atmo and the artificial gravity of the ship kicked in. Three minutes after takeoff, Night announced they'd cleared the planet and were heading out of Dominion territory.

They were as safe as they could be.

For now.

She squeezed Storm's hand and gave him a smile. Then she forced a serious expression. "We're safe. So now you need to tell me how I shot fire out of my hands."

HOW WAS he supposed to tell this woman that she was his mate and held the key to all his future happiness in her hands? The stories of fated matings made it sound easier.

Storm had never been more terrified in his life.

"Let's find someplace private to talk," he suggested. He didn't want anyone from either delegation walking in on this conversation.

Finding a room bought him a minute as he scrambled to think of the right words to say. He led her down the hall. He could hear Echo and Rush speaking quietly to one another further down the way.

Doors lined this hallway and Storm tried the first one. It wasn't locked, and inside it led to a small room meant to be shared by two soldiers. From the looks of it, this one hadn't been used by the mercenaries, and he was thankful for that. He didn't want the ghosts of the men they'd fought haunting this conversation.

There were no sheets on the small cot that was connected to the wall. The whole place had an unused feeling to it. There wasn't even any dust on the surfaces.

River sat on the cot and looked up at him. "Is this private enough for you?" There was a wary edge to her voice. "What's going on, Storm? Is something wrong with me? Is that why I could do… that? Am I some… I don't even know." She crossed her arms and hugged herself.

That wouldn't do at all. He sat beside her, wanting desperately to reach out and hold her, but not yet. Not until she knew the truth. It was the only way to move forward.

And there was no stalling anymore. "You can wield my fire because you're my mate."

There. He'd said it. It was out in the open. He let out a pent up breath, but still balanced on a knife's edge of terror. This was the moment she could reject him once and for all, where she could push him away for lying to her for days while their lives depended on honesty.

Really, what in the stars had he been thinking?

River was looking at him, eyes wide and unblinking. Then she blinked hard and shook her head. "What?"

He reached out and took her hand, rubbing his palm over the back of hers. "You're my fated mate. Yesterday, while I flew, I could hear your thoughts in my head. That was the first sign." Was that really only yesterday? A lifetime of action had happened since then, but time had a funny way of expanding and contracting when things were really important. "And then last night, I knew for certain when you held my flame in your hands. It would have burned anyone who wasn't my mate, even another dragon."

"You were willing to burn me?" She pulled her hand away.

He let her go. "I have a bit more control than that. I would have banished my flame before you felt anything worse than a pinch. But you didn't." He turned himself until he was fully facing her, one hand planted on the cot and the other resting on his thigh but straining to reach out for her. "I didn't come on this mission to meet you. I was a total fool. But from the moment I saw you, I wanted you. If nothing else, can you feel that?" If he were a little bolder, he might have reached for her hand again and showed her exactly what she did to him. But the chances of a backfire were huge. River held her emotions close and he didn't know if she was amazed, horrified, or somewhere in between.

She gulped. "Is this the part where you tell me you're dragging me home to your castle or whatever and I'll be your mate whether I like it or not?" There was a bit of strained humor in the question.

"It's not really a castle, just a big house." Her eyes got impossibly wider, and Storm couldn't help grinning. He reached up and cupped her cheek. "I want to be near you. I want to give this thing between us a chance to blossom. And I would love to show you Vemion. But I'm not asking you to pledge your undying love for me just yet. I know this is new." New, maybe, but he knew what he felt, and he knew it would only deepen with time. But today was, perhaps, a day for just one revelation.

"What are you asking me to do?" She hadn't pulled away from his embrace, and she was meeting his eyes head on.

Good signs.

"Just a kiss." He wanted to lean forward and capture her lips, to take her right there and show her exactly what a dragon lord could do. But she needed to make this move, to take this first step to accepting him.

River let her eyes drift shut, leaned forward, and covered his lips with her own. It was gentle, an exploration that he let himself sink into.

His arm slid to wrap around her and pull her close as the kiss deepened, her mouth opening to let him in. His tongue slid past her teeth to tangle with hers, and she made a soft sound in the back of her throat.

Her hand came up to fist in his shirt as she pulled

him closer, the position a bit awkward from the way that they were sitting, but he didn't care, not with the taste of River on his tongue.

Desire surged in him, his cock hardening as his senses overwhelmed him. This was his mate, right here in his arms, kissing him like he could conquer the world, like he was some kind of hero.

Like she was his.

Storm groaned into her mouth. He was a dragon lord. Anything he wanted was his for the taking. And yet all that he now craved was in her hands.

Her hand trailed down and landed on the button of his trousers. He trembled at the promise of that light touch, his cock straining to be freed. It was nothing more than a whisper of her fingers, but his entire being was focused on the feel of her.

River slowly unfastened his pants with an unskillful hand, needing to pull away for a moment to look down and see what she was doing. Confidence returned as she slid her hand inside, gripping him tightly as she stroked up and down.

He covered her mouth with his again as the sensation overwhelmed him. He gasped into her mouth, groaning low in his throat. He thrust up into her, that simple touch enough to nearly make him spill.

He wouldn't. Not this first time, not when he finally had her. He moved suddenly, pulling away from her hand with true regret and laying her down gently on the cot. He loomed over her and saw a heat in her eyes that matched his own.

"You know, I wanted you from the moment I saw you, too," she said. Her breaths weren't even, and she arched up into his touch as he slowly slid his hand under her shirt and teased the soft skin under it. "I don't know about this mate stuff, but I know that."

He could work with that. He pressed down onto her, careful not to crush her with his weight, and kissed her again.

Storm gave himself over to her pleasure as his lips teased hers open, as his tongue stroked into her mouth. She gasped and he took advantage, deepening the kiss. He wanted to spend a day doing nothing but kissing his mate, thrusting her to the very heights of pleasure with only the meeting of lips and tongue. It would drive them both mad with lust and he'd spend the next day buried deep inside of her.

Once he had her, he was never letting go.

He let his lips trail her jaw and down her neck to the sensitive spot just below her ear, then he tugged on her earlobe with his teeth until she gasped. "I'm going to pleasure you now," he whispered, certain his voice rumbled through her entire body. "Let me taste you."

River moaned and nodded against him. She pushed him down her body with one hand even as her lips sought his out for another kiss.

Storm was powerless to do anything but take her

kiss. What kind of dragon would he be if he rejected his mate's touch?

He wasn't about to find out.

But he didn't let himself get lost in this kiss, determined instead to bring his mate to the heights of pleasure before he slaked his own lust inside of her.

Her pants slid off with ease and she tossed her own shirt aside, leaving herself bare to him. Storm stared, heat surging through him. This woman was his, destined by fate and proven by fire.

And he was going to claim her.

He spread her legs and kissed her thighs, slowly making his way up to her heated sex. She was ready for him, the scent of her enveloping him as pleasure dripped from her and tempted his lips.

He wanted to devour her, a dragon with his prize. But he forced himself to be gentle, teasing her as he did so, letting the tip of his tongue slide along her slit. She moaned loudly as he teased her sex.

He wanted everything from her, and he was determined to give her everything in return. He eased one finger inside of her, and he could feel her body respond, tight and ready and nearing the edge he was leading her toward.

He needed her to shatter, for her to be swept away in a wave of pleasure so great it ruined her for anyone but him. Because he wasn't letting his mate walk away.

She gasped out his name as her orgasm took her,

her body rippling around his fingers in a promise of pleasure he didn't want to resist. He soothed her through it, his fingers and tongue taking her even as she writhed there on that dingy cot and lost all awareness of where she was.

He needed inside of her. It was an imperative. He was certain he'd go mad if he didn't take her right then.

River blinked open lust drunk eyes as he kissed his way back up her stomach and loomed over her. "You're still wearing clothes."

If he wasn't so desperate, he might have followed her implied invitation and stripped, but his cock was out, his pants shoved down to give him enough room to maneuver.

"Later," he promised. "Need you now." Then he guided himself to her entrance and had to bite back a groan as he slid in.

This was what he'd been waiting for his entire life, the promise of his mate hot, wet, and gasping around him as he filled her.

River's eyes were wide as she watched him sink deep into her. Her fingers gripped his arms, her nails leaving the promises of marks in his skin. He wanted to be marked by her, wanted all to know that he was as much hers as she was his. He wanted her name tattooed on his throat. He wanted to cover her in his gold and jewels so there was no mistaking their bond.

But right then, he just needed her.

He couldn't stop himself from moving his body, thrusting into her. And River met his every move. He might have only discovered she was his mate the day before, but how had he resisted for even those hours?

This was paradise.

The need for more over took him and he drove himself into her, his thrusts growing harder, more urgent as she moaned beneath him. Her body clenched around him, tight and wet and perfect. He could feel the edge coming closer, but he didn't stop.

He wanted to make her scream in pleasure, wanted to know that she was lost in this moment just as much as he was. He was lost in a haze of pleasure, only aware of the ripples of ecstasy that pulsed through his mate's body with every movement as he took her over the edge again. He fucked her hard, unable to control himself as he drove into her, and finally, as she came around him, he emptied himself into her, vision going hazy with the thrill of it all.

Time drifted for a bit after that as they clutched one another close. River shivered, the air around them probably uncomfortable on her naked body. Storm pulled her close to him and nuzzled against her neck.

He wanted to make promises to her, wanted her to know that she'd always be safe with him, always come first in his heart.

But she hadn't offered him anything more than this moment. She knew he was his mate. She knew he wanted more of her. But she would still have to accept him.

River groaned and sat up, eyes darting around the little room for her discarded clothes. "I'm not sure how long we'll be on this ship, but you're welcome to bunk with me until..." She looked away, not finishing the sentence.

He knew. Until their people came to collect them. Until they were torn apart.

"There are humans on Vemion," he offered, in case that was part of her objection. "Two of my cousins have human mates."

"Cousins? Other dragon lords?" It wasn't the response he was hoping for. In fact, she sounded a bit panicked.

He'd throw away his title in a heartbeat if she demanded it. He might have already, in his rush to claim her. He'd forgotten his mother's ultimatum in all the excitement. But he'd never planned to give in to her demands anyway. And he wouldn't sacrifice River for anything.

"They're princes, actually. Their father is the king of Vemion."

"Your uncle?" Her voice went so high on that word it ended in a squeak. She quickly pulled on her clothes. "Uh, right, um..." She cleared her throat and looked around the room, but he didn't know what she could be looking for. It was empty except for the two of them. "I think we should go find the others."

So his family would be a problem. It could be dealt with. Once she met them, she'd understand they were no different than anyone else. And there were advantages to being mated to a rich dragon lord.

He stood and readjusted his clothes, well aware of how rumpled they must have looked. One glance at the two of them and it would be clear what had happened. Storm was tempted to puff out his chest and declare it to all. He wanted everyone to know he belonged to this amazing woman.

River's eyes flicked up and down, taking him in, and her cheeks flamed. Whether reliving the memory of what they'd just done or in the knowledge that he looked so satisfied, he wasn't sure. But she didn't say anything, instead spinning around and opening the door.

As they walked into the hallway, the human leader Seth happened to be passing by. He looked at River, then to Storm. And his lips pulled into a strangely satisfied smile.

"You've done well, River. I'd say we can call this mission a success."

What was that supposed to mean?

Before Storm could figure out what the human was talking about, River made a sound in the back of her throat and took off running.

RIVER RAN BLINDLY through the ship, needing to get away from Seth.

And Storm.

What must he think of her? To make love to her like that and then hear that it was all some sort of ruse? A success? They'd nearly been killed by mercenaries! The only thing that had gone right was that River had found Storm. She'd forgotten about Seth's instructions, the need to get close to the dragon.

No, that had happened all on its own.

She didn't know it was possible to fall for someone in two days. Or maybe it had been coming on slowly over the course of the two weeks they'd been at the compound before the attack. Whatever it was, she'd been ecstatic when Storm revealed exactly what she meant to him.

Ecstatic and terrified.

Her life was spinning fast, opportunities in all directions. Or failures. Could she really expect more diplomatic jobs after the failure of this mission? Or would she be hailed as a hero and given whatever position she wanted for her instrumental part in saving the day?

Maybe none of that would happen. Maybe she'd simply go back to Mayt and resume her old life as if nothing had happened. As if she hadn't taken on mercenaries and found out she was a dragon's mate.

Footsteps echoed in the hallway behind her. River darted into a nearby room, the need to hide driving her.

It was another bedroom, but here both cots were folded up and secured to the wall. The rest of the room was barren. She closed the door but couldn't see the locking mechanism. Whatever. It was fine.

River clutched at her hair and had to bite back a primal scream. She was supposed to be safe now, so why did it feel like everything was falling apart?

A knock on the door echoed through the metal of the room all around her.

River stared at the door like it might bite her. She slowly lowered her hands and took several breaths. She didn't want to face anyone. She didn't want to deal with anything. She just wanted to disappear and magically reappear back home where everything made sense.

Of course, that would be a problem since she wouldn't have Storm.

Another knock echoed.

If it was Seth, he'd be banging on the door or barging in without an invite. He wasn't the type to follow her anyway. He thought he'd got what he wanted.

She took another deep breath and opened the door, unsurprised to see Storm standing there.

"May I come in?" he asked.

She stepped aside to let him in and then let the door slide shut. Storm was quiet for several moments, giving her the opportunity to speak first. But when she didn't, he did. "Are you alright?"

"Seth told me I should seduce you." She blurted it, and the second the words were out, she wanted to pull them back.

Storm blinked several times. "What we just did had nothing to do with Seth." It wasn't a question.

"Of course not." She hugged herself and wished the room was a bit bigger. This was the perfect time for pacing. "It's just that he was right there, right after we did *that*. And... I don't know. It kind of broke my brain."

Arms wrapped around her, the warm feel of her dragon mate holding her close. He kissed her hair and swayed back and forth. "It's alright. It's been an exciting few days."

"That's one way of putting it." If she was never excited again, it would be too soon. She squirmed until she could free her own arms and wrap them back around Storm. It felt good to just *be*, safe for once without mercenaries or drones or anything threatening them.

So why couldn't she convince her brain everything was fine?

"It's not just Seth." Maybe talking would help. Of the two of them, Storm was much more experienced with combat. He knew how to calm a person down.

"What is it?"

"I feel like we got off too easy. Like rescuing everyone should have been more difficult." She could still imagine the weight of the blaster in her hands, and she'd be seeing the men she shot until the day she died.

"Easy?" He pulled back and looked down at her, eyebrows raised. "A building exploded."

"A building we infiltrated like it was empty. And I'm still trying to figure out who called the hit. I *know* how Mayt works. Not everyone is in favor of this negotiation. Some people think dragons are ferocious beasts who can't be reasoned with."

"Rude." He smiled as he said it.

River stepped out of his arms, regretting the loss of him even as she did it. But she needed to think. "We're on the mercenaries' ship. They were probably paid a great deal of money to do this. And there aren't that many people on Mayt who could afford it."

"Do you think there's a failsafe of some kind? Something besides the bomb?" He was taking her seriously. That only made the anxiety simmering within her worse.

"I'm worried they might have one. Someone wanted Seth dead badly enough to hire twenty mercenaries. They were willing to kill all of us. This just doesn't feel over." She didn't feel any safer for having said it, but a weight had lifted off her shoulders. Now she wasn't the only one thinking her thoughts. "I think we should have a guard on Seth until we're sure we're safe. Just in case."

Just in case one of her own people wanted to hurt him. She couldn't quite manage to say that out loud, but Storm was already nodding.

"Let's go."

They ran through the narrow halls of the ship, and it felt like the entire place had doubled in size. It was probably the panic talking, and River tried to ignore it. Storm took the lead, and after a minute, she realized they were heading for the cockpit.

Made sense. If someone wanted to control the ship, that was where they'd do it.

They skidded to a stop to let the door open, and when it did, River at first didn't understand what she was looking at. And then it clicked into place with stunning clarity.

One of the dragons was crumpled on the floor, a nasty welt on his head. Seth was backed up against one wall, his hands up and face a wash of terror.

And Luke Zeal was pointing a blaster straight at him.

Luke started to turn their way as the door opened, then *everyone* moved. Despite the blaster, Storm lunged forward. Seth burst off the wall, launching himself at Luke from the side. And River was left there, slightly behind Storm and unable to act.

She pressed the control to slide the door closed. At least she could stop Luke from getting away.

Two on one, especially with an angry dragon in the fight, meant that Luke didn't stand a chance. Storm got a hold of his hand and pressed hard until it released the blaster, which he swatted out of Luke's reach.

"Why?" Seth was demanding. "What were you planning?"

"They're a danger to us all," Luke declared defiantly. "They'll take us as slaves and steal our planet. We can't negotiate with them. Learn your history."

While Luke raved, River checked on the fallen dragon and was relieved to see that he was breathing. She pulled the first aid kit off the wall and started applying med gel to the nasty wound on his head.

It didn't take long for the rest of the party to make

its way to the cockpit. Shock rippled through them when they found Luke tied up and Seth now holding the blaster. He didn't point it at the man, but he was clearly ready to do damage if he had to.

"We need to call our people," Seth said. "And find a holding cell for this one. I think we've found who hired the mercenaries."

Everything seemed to happen in a blink after that. The calls were made, Luke was imprisoned, and all they had to do was wait for their rescue.

And finally, River let herself believe she was safe.

So why did her heart start beating fast when Storm found her an hour later?

She was sitting in a small area with padded seats and an entertainment screen embedded in the wall, trying to make sense of all that had happened. She doubted she would ever completely understand. She didn't have it in her to plot a murder.

"We received word from Vemion and Mayt. Both should be arriving within a few hours. Seth has requested that this ship be remanded to Mayt. Rush agreed." He reached for her hand and tangled their fingers together.

She squeezed. "So that's it?"

"Almost."

"Yeah?" She couldn't let him go. It was crazy to think that after only two days, but it was a truth she could feel deep in her soul.

"Come home with me," Storm asked. "See what it's like to be my mate. Give this a chance. Please."

It was absolutely crazy. But River couldn't help the smile that bloomed on her face as she nodded. "I can't wait to see it."

EPILOGUE

ONE YEAR *Later*

River clutched at Storm's scales and whooped with joy as he swooped down, the wind whipping through her hair. It was cold this high up, but elation kept her warm. Not to mention that her mate was a furnace, even in this form.

She could feel what he planned to do even before she heard his voice in her head. *Ready? Hold on!*

He didn't give her a chance to object, flipping over in a barrel roll and righting himself before she fell off and plummeted to the ground.

In all their rides, she hadn't lost her seat yet.

They flew out over the roiling sea and River couldn't help but wonder at the fact that this was her home now, this beautiful and wild place filled with dragons. She'd thought she'd need time to adjust.

Instead, she'd fallen in love at first sight.

Storm turned back before they went too far and landed at the edge of their estate. Once she dismounted, he shifted back to his human form and held out his hand for her. She took it eagerly and greeted him with a kiss.

"Today is the day," she said, forcing the smile to stay on her face.

Not every day had been smiles and happiness since her return. After she'd been here a month, Storm had let her know about his mother's ultimatum: find a suitable bride or lose his inheritance.

She and her mate wouldn't exactly be destitute if his mother disowned him, but she knew it would hurt. And not just because of their money. Storm didn't say it, but he didn't want his mother to reject him.

River had her own thoughts about her dragon-in-law, but she kept them to herself. She was here to support her mate. It didn't mean she would roll over and take his mother's insults, but she wasn't going to start a fight either.

"We could just stay home. Get a fire going. Lounge around in bed." He pulled her in closer so he could put an arm around her shoulders.

"Tempting, but would you really leave Cipher and Drake to deal with that? Especially with…" She didn't want to get into his mother's potential issues with his brothers. That way led to even more craziness.

"If she says anything about you…"

"I know, my dear mate." She landed a sloppy kiss on his cheek. "But use some of those diplomatic skills and be the bigger dragon."

"Most diplomatic missions don't end with double digit body counts." Storm hadn't seemed eager to take up another diplomatic job, and River couldn't blame him. Recently she'd found work as an administrator in a local school where Storm volunteered with the children. They were both better suited to schoolwork rather than diplomacy.

She didn't want to dwell on the body count. Sometimes she woke up with nightmares. But Storm was always there to soothe them away.

"Our ride will be here soon. You have just enough time to change your clothes." They approached the large stone stairway that led into the house, and it no longer felt surreal that she lived in a dragon's mansion on his grand estate.

Funny what a girl could get used to.

Storm tried to pull her along with him. "Help me choose an outfit."

"If I go into your dressing room with you, we'll be late." She leaned in and kissed him again, forcing herself to pull away before it deepened. "Now go. If you're not ready in time, I'll use you as an example of tardiness at the school next week. All those kids will know you messed up."

Her mate laughed, but he headed for his dressing room. And he joined her once more, just in time. Their vehicle was waiting on the road out front, and his mother was due to get off her shuttle in less than an hour.

"Whatever happens, I'm with you," Storm assured her.

"That's my line." At first, she might have been worried about what his mother's rejection might have meant for them. Now River had had a year to be secure in her position and her mate's love. "Let's get this over with. Then you can tell me exactly what you plan to do once you get me back in bed."

Thank you for reading *Storm*!
The series continues with Drake.

WHAT TO READ NEXT: DRAKE

Danger stalks a downed ship in an alien jungle…

When Drake receive a distress call from a nearby planet he has to respond. People need help, and it allows him to focus on something other than the devastating news delivered by the Royal Matchmaker. But he can't believes what he finds when he and his crew discover the survivors.

She's on the adventure of a lifetime…

Claudia might have been born a simple Earth girl, but she's spent the last few years traversing the discovery and seeing things people back home would never believe. But she doesn't want to end up as monster chow on an alien planet. When Drake arrives, she lets herself believe they just might escape.

But an invisible monster is hunting them. How can the fight a monster they can't see? She needs to focus on survival, but she can't take her eyes off the way-too-hot dragon who's stealing all her attention.

If they can survive the monster, does a simple Earth girl have any chance at keeping a dragon's heart?

Check it out!

INTERGALACTIC DATING AGENCY

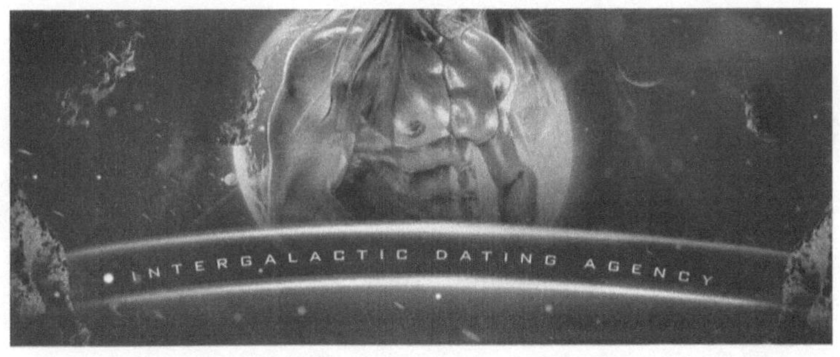

LOOKING for love that's out of this world? These strong, smart, sexy aliens are seeking mates from the Milky Way. Just hop onboard with your local Intergalactic Dating Agency. Join our group of authors as we explore the friendly skies and beyond with trilogies of cosmic craving, astral adventure, and otherworldly lovers. Warning: abductions may or may not be included!

ALSO BY KATE RUDOLPH

Looking for something else? Kate Rudolph has a heart pounding collection or paranormal and sci-fi romance stories for you! Bundles, bears, audiobooks, aliens, and more. Check out your options in the list below. You can find out all you need to know at www.katerudolph.net.

Want to check out one of the books? Click on the series name to find out more!

Dragon Brides

Fated mates, fierce women, and dragon princes.

Also available in audio!

Crux

Ranger

Saber

Cipher

Storm

Drake

———

Alien Mates: Planet Exile

Guerran is no place for pretty human women. But these alien heroes will protect their mates!

Also available in audio!

Exile's Hunter

Exile's Adored

Zulir Warrior Mates

Kidnapped humans. Alien Warriors. Electric wings.

The Zulir Warrior Mates series brings you human heroines and heroes abducted from Earth who find love – and wings! – with the alien warriors who rescue them.

Also available in audio!

Synnr's Saint

Synnr's Hope

Synnr's Spark

Synnr's Kiss

Guarded by the Shifter

Werewolf. Bodyguard. Mate.

The origins of these shifters are shrouded in mystery, but they're determined to protect their mates from any harm that comes their way.

Also available in audio!

Hunting Season

On the Prowl

Stalking Magic

Hungry for the Wolf

———

Detyen Warriors

Detya was destroyed a hundred years ago. These doomed warriors are out to find justice… and their mates.

The Detyen Warriors series brings you kick butt heroines, alpha alien heroes, fated mates, and relationships strong enough to span the galaxy!

The entire series is also available in audio!

Soulless

Ruthless

Heartless

Faultless

Endless

———

Alien Holiday Romance

Christmas… in space????

These alien holiday romances look beyond Earth's winter holidays and ring in the season across the galaxy! *Select titles available in audio.*

Snowed in with the Alien Beast

The Alien's Winter Gift

The Alien Reindeer's Wild Ride

Trapped with her Alien Mate

———

Alien Outlaws

Outlaws, schemes, and love… it's all there in the Alien Outlaws series…

Andie Munster is sick of life on Ixilta, the planet she got dumped on after being abducted from Earth six years ago. And when the mysterious and dangerous Xandr shows up looking for a way off the planet, she's half-prisoner, half-co-conspirator in a wild rush to escape.

Rogue Alien's Escape

Rogue Alien's Woman

Rogue Alien's Secret

Rogue Alien's Legacy

Mated to the Alien

Fated Mate Alien Romance

Detyens are doomed to die young if they don't find their fated mates.

Follow along as these mated pairs fight off aliens, corrupt dictators, prejudiced humans, pirates, and more! The books can be read or listened to in any order, though some characters show up in multiple stories.

Select books available in audio.

Pick a book and jump into the action today!

Ruwen

Tyral

Stoan

Cyborg

Krayter

Kayleb

Shayn

Braxtyn

Doryan

Dekon

Stealing the Alpha

The thief takes what she wants, but the alpha keeps what's his...

Join shifter thief Mel as she clashes with lion alpha Luke in an explosive trilogy of two opposites who can't keep away from one another.

Also available in audio!

The Alpha Heist

Entangled with the Thief

In the Alpha's Bed

————

Save with box sets!

Aliens. Shifters. Warriors. Mates. Get them all wrapped together in these special box sets. Save up to 30% off the price of buying the individual books, depending on the series!

Alien Outlaws: The Complete Series

Mated to the Alien Volume One (also available in audio)

Mated to the Alien Volume Two (also available in audio)

Mated to the Alien Volume Three

Mated to the Alien Volume Four

Stealing the Alpha: The Complete Series (also available in audio)

The Mate Bundle

Detyen Warriors Volume One (also available in audio)

Detyen Warriors Volume Two (also available in audio)

Zulir Warrior Mates Volume One (also available in audio)

Standalone Paranormal and Sci-Fi Romance:

Crashed

Mated on the Moon

Mated to the Alien Dragon

Marked

Bear in Mind

Alpha's Mercy

Gemma's Mate

Find more by Kate Rudolph at www.katerudolph.net

ABOUT KATE RUDOLPH

KATE RUDOLPH IS paranormal and sci-fi romance writer who lives in Indiana. She loves writing about kick butt heroines and the steamy heroes who love them. She's been devouring romance novels since she was too young to be reading them and had to hide her books so no one would take them away. She couldn't imagine a better job in this world than writing romances and sharing them with her fellow readers.

If you enjoyed this story, please consider leaving a review.

www.ingramcontent.com/pod-product-compliance
Lightning Source LLC
Chambersburg PA
CBHW030640190726
48286CB00008B/2594